DEŁMAR

OF THE

DEEPS

DELMAR
OF THE
DEEPS

For Noel

Nino Balistreri

Nino Balistreri

Cover: Griffon Studio Arthouse

National Library of Canada Cataloguing in Publication

Caruso, Anthony, 1944-

     Lauderdale Tales / Nino Balistreri

ISBN 978-1-7750849-4-5

       Fiction > Gay

       Fiction > Lesbian

Prologue

My name is Ennis, my father's name is Jasper and my mother's name is Delja. My father and I do have a last name. It's a common name from where we come from, the West coast of England. There is nothing wrong with our family name but out of respect for my mother and her family we seldom use it. You see she is from another place, a place where by ancient tradition everyone has a first name only and no need for a formal second name.

I was lovingly raised from the day of my birth by my father and my grandmother, his mother. It was not because I was abandoned at birth by my mother, but because it would have been fatal for me to stay in her care.

As I grew, each year from mid spring to mid fall I spent a lot of days with my mother and her family. But sadly I only spent my days. Because of where she lived, I was never able to as the term goes 'sleep over'.

What you are about to read is the story of my parents enduring love and more importantly, the story of my mother's people and their connection to an incredible world that we can only imagine.

It was during my secondary education that I had an English teacher who lauded my writing skills. I must confess that I did well in writing about the subjects that were assigned, but when it came to creating on my own, my imagination failed me.

One day my English teacher had a talk with me regarding a free choice fiction writing assignment. I knew that it was not good, certainly not up to the quality of the topics that I was assigned to write about.

After a long discussion my teacher came to a conclusion. She suggested that I write about what I know rather than creating fiction on a subject that I was unable to relate to.

That night I had a long talk with my father. I told him about an idea that I had fostered in the back of my mind for many years now. At first he was shocked and definitely against me writing about the subject. You see, the subject was the story of my life and my father's loving relationship with my mother and her people.

Because of making my idea known, things were tense at home for a few days. Dad and I talked a lot, we are very close. When we spend special times talking about the important matters of our lives, dad always cradles me in his arms. As long as we both shall live, this will never change.

You see, it is the way of my mothers people to convey all their emotions by using intimate body contact. In other words, all social emotions are conveyed by her people by tactile connections. Friendship, caring, happiness and of course love. Be it platonic or sexual, her people accept body contact as a natural part of their psyche.

After much discussion my father and I came to a decision. It was now early spring. I would wait a few weeks until my mother arrived for the summer season. I will talk about my idea with her and have her talk it over with her family and community elders.

If, and only if, I am given permission, I will begin my story. It will be a slow process because I will have to interview her elders and many people in her community. Added to the process will be the near impossible task of translating what they communicate to me into my language. Her language does not have an actual vocabulary. I come by the ability to converse with my mother because her communication skills were ingrained into my being at birth.

I anxiously awaited my mother's arrival that spring. I decided to not hit her with my idea on our first day together. I obviously underestimated her emotional skills. By half way through the day she drew her partner Zeeman to her side and together they held me tightly in their usual loving embrace. She looked deep into my eyes and expressed to me that I was harbouring something inside that I needed to get out.

As always, her instincts were correct. It took a while to express in her language, but I persisted. When I finished, both her and Zeeman were obviously in shock. I comforted them both while continually assuring them that my intentions were loving. I also assured them that if her family and elders refused me permission, I would not attempt to write my story.

I expressed to my mother that I was already well versed in how to keep the secrets of her family and life to myself, only sharing with my dad. I didn't know if my grandmother knew the truth of my mother and never asked.

The process took most of that summer and early fall season. Once the elders gave my mother tentative approval, I was assigned to Jennis, a younger member of the elders council. Jennis was a magnificent specimen if maleness, one that I could only dream of being. I am tall and more than fit. But in stature I take after my father rather than my mother's side of the family.

It took many days that season for Jennis to convey the story of his people. The currents were warm that summer so I never chilled. I was certainly comfortable floating in Jennis's arms for hours at a time. I kept a pad secured to the gunnels of my boat in order to make notes and record the many names as Jennis conveyed his peoples story to me.

Each time I leaned over the boats gunnel to write Jennis held me tight in place while watching in fascination as I moved my pencil over the pages. For whatever reason I only realized that day that my mother's people only kept an oral history and had never developed the need to physically record facts.

When Jennis gave me his feelings for both his mating and life partners and many of his peoples intimate traditions he often became aroused. At first he was embarrassed because it was not sexual excitement aimed at me. When I caressed him and showed him that the sensual aspects of his story were also causing me to have involuntary erections and on a couple of occasions involuntary orgasms he relaxed and smiled.

Jennis confessed that he had been fighting against having orgasms over his recollections for fear of upsetting me. After that day we celebrated our rigid reactions and laughed when we each experienced involuntary orgasms. Like his people's traditions, these functions are just part of their makeup. We were both young virile adults and I loved the fact that with Jennis, I could relax and enjoy the sensations that my body was experiencing without it being a sexual experience.

I hope that you will take away from this story an enhanced love of the oceans and the importance of protecting them from the practices that destroy.

1

Bahari floated, barely flexing his muscular torso and fins, as he watched the young play happily in the surging current. This light was bright and calm. The waters had warmed, making every member of the Delmar pod feel happy. Entire schools of small sea creatures moved in vast numbers above, through and around the large underwater gathering. Most of the small creatures traveled in extremely tight formation, totally ignoring the Delmar. Others, being tamer and possessing a more curious nature, drew in near, closely examining the activities that were taking place.

Like many of his kind, Bahari was familiar with these more friendly creatures, often playing with and caressing them. It was especially pleasing for the little Delmar spawn. They loved to tease and touch their tiny ocean friends. They thought it a wonderful game, when the creatures playfully swam through and nibbled at their flowing hair. Unknown to the little ones, the small creatures loved to search through their floating tresses, in hopes of finding minute bits of edible sea life caught up in their long silky strands.

Bahari was pleased. The world of the Delmar was a joyous one this light. Everyone was well. The older youthful spawn, independent of their breeding life-givers, today played their favorite game. Each in turn was circling around and then positioning themselves, in close to an ancient stone wall. Nearing the wall, the fast warm current funneled and enveloped them. With minimal flexing of their strong lithe bodies, the waters surge propelled the youthful spawn, to gleefully twirl and tumble in and out, through a series of ancient pillars and archways.

To the young Delmar, this was simply a favorite play place. But like the elders, Bahari was aware of its past existence. Many generations ago, this was a dry place, resting high above their watery world. Then it was inhabited by creatures not totally unlike themselves.

But in dramatic ways, they were different from the Delmar. As the Delmar called them, 'The dry place creatures' They had strange looking flesh covered columns, supporting them upright. Unlike his kind, whose lower half consisted of a solid mass of muscles, covered in sturdy scales. Their flesh covered pillars allowed these creatures to move about most efficiently on the dry places, but less so on the surface of the Delmar's watery domain.

Strangely, from the mid section upwards, they were more visibly similar. He had observed the creatures at play, while afloat upon the surface of his world. When the males entered the watery domain to bathe, they acted differently. Either alone or in groups, they more often than not removed most or all of the strange articles, covering their forms.

Carefully observing from below, Bahari and other Delmar could see that the males had different degrees of hair covering their shapes. They also had varied patterns, color and thickness of hair, surrounding their breeding members. Similarly, on rare occasions, they observed the female of the species. The females had little or no hair on their structures, but strangely, their breeding access was completely hidden behind a matted covering.

He and all Delmar males agreed. It looked unnatural to see all that flesh. Although it seemed to be in many shades, depending on the creature, they all had at least, a similar area of hair encompassing their coupling areas. They found it amusing. When these male creatures cavorted and played in the water. Unlike the Delmar males, these pillared ones did not seem to be aware, or possibly didn't care about appearances. When exerting themselves, their breeding appendages were often fully engorged, standing out most of the time.

One other major difference was evident, when these creatures let their hair flow back. They had varied, but at the same time, similar shapes of flesh, protruding from the sides of their heads. Bahari believed that these flesh growths were a means of detecting sounds. Elders confirmed this when asked. But they knew from passed on experience, these sound sensing openings on the creatures heads, were extremely basic. They could not detect natural water borne tones. These were subtle vibrations, the Delmar and many other creatures of the watery deeps emanated, for long distance communication.

Without fail, it was the same, each time the Delmar observed the pillared creatures at play. The Delmar water-borne sensitivity to sounds, made the extremely loud sounds of the pillared ones difficult to bear. The benefit derived from withstanding the high pitch sounds was anonymity. It allowed the Delmar hovering below; to communicate at will, with no fear of detection.

Bahari like all of the males of his kind, had layers of flesh like vents just below the hair line on each side of his head. These vents opened and closed naturally, allowing water to flow through from their mouths. From this continuous flow, the Delmar filtered and ingested much of their life sustaining needs. Inset deep within these vents, they possessed powerful senses. These gave them the ability to hear, as well, allow them to feel the deep low sounds. These tones were detected rather than heard. They were inner sensations, traveling through the ocean currents, from the far reaches of their watery domain.

The males of the deep were entirely devoid of body hair. Only their heads bore long flowing tresses of varying colors. This, Bahari knew, was an inherited trait, passed on from their breeding life givers.

Both male and female Delmar protected their reproductive organs, neatly and securely enfolded in layers of heavy scaly tissue. This scaly tissue covered all Delmar bodies, from just below their middle, to the beginning of their large fan like maneuvering appendage.

Observing the often feeble craft of the pillared ones, afloat upon the surface was an education. It was obvious to Bahari and all Delmar that the pillared creatures could not survive beneath the waves of his watery domain. Many times in his adult life, Bahari had assisted other Delmar males. They learned to move under these creatures, bearing them up, after their floating structures floundered in raging waters. It was a difficult maneuver, taught to each mature spawn, by his nurturing male or life-giver.

On these occasions, they bore up and carried the distressed creatures, towards the nearest dry place. Most importantly, it was necessary at all times to take care not to be detected. The pillared creatures had to believe, that the surging waves bore them up, rescuing them. It was taught to all ages of Delmar society. To become known would have brought on many sorrows and a real danger of death for their undersea gathering, along with the probable extinction of all Delmar pods who existed in the great waters.

Sadly, there were, more often than not, just too many creatures to bear up. Or their craft floundered too great a distance from a dry safe place. When this happened, Delmar tradition dictated their actions. On these sad occasions, the society of Elders and adult males gathered together. As a community they took care to convey these lifeless creatures to a peaceful resting place, deep below the waves.

The Delmar lived by a kindly rule that believed in love for all. Although they recognized the dry place creatures as being dangerous to their existence, it was not in their nature to wish them harm. As a loving and caring community, they were raised to look out for the well being of all creatures, be they of their realm, or of the air breathing places. The harsh realities of life, death and suffering, were an ingrained part of their societies knowledge.

Having observed the pillared ones for much of his thirty cycles, Bahari wished that they could all live in unison, fully aware of each other's existence. Being from the realm of the deep, the Delmar had the ability to assist the dry creatures in so many ways. But Bahari knew from generations of gathered experience that the pillared ones would not understand their society.

Elders assured all Delmar generations that interaction with these dry creatures could only end in sorrow and tragedy for all. The giant air breathing inhabitants of their water world were a prime example. They were so passive and kind, loving life and all existence that thrived above and below the waves.

Like the Delmar it was also their nature to be unable to bear anger, hatred or violence against any creature that they shared their existence with.

Unlike the Delmar, they did not differentiate between land and water creatures. They loved all existence. It was unfortunately their common belief that they could co-exist in peace, alongside the surface creatures. To their dismay, the dry place creatures took advantage of their friendship and docility. They plied the waters in every sector of their domains, to capture and slaughter the gentle giants.

2

Today's gathering was a special one. The cold dark time was ending. Every new light felt warmer, bringing with it continually gentler currents.

The Delmar pod as a whole had returned to their favorite place of rest in just in the last eight lights. It was not as colorful in flora or its edibles. It did not boast the brilliant rainbow of florescent creatures from their warmer place. Their time far away in the tropical water was always enjoyable and vibrant. But there was an excitement for both the male and female Delmar, to return with the warming waters, to their breeding home. Rarely did a Delmar female enter into a breeding state, during the tropical water part of their cycle.

Bahari was not alone today, watching the young at play. His breeding partner was by his side. Yahaira had brought two of their three female spawn, to play with their male offspring. Together their spawn would enjoy today's festival of warming waters. Yahaira's life partner Gryta stayed back this light. She was helping to care for the collective female spawn that were too tiny to take part in the festival. Bahari and Yahara had brought forth three female spawn. The eldest spawn's sound was Larina. Then they had Lanikai and finally their youngest female spawn carried the sound Lulwa. They had also produced three male spawn. The eldest two now in Bahari's care were given the sounds Dylon and the youngest male Zamar.

Dylon, the eldest of Bahari's spawn, was fast approaching his cycle when he would enter the reproductive stream. Being just three cycles old, Zamar was safely enfolded in Bahari's strong arms enjoying the excitement as his older siblings participated in the activities of the festival.

This interaction of their collective spawn did not happen often, just three or four festival lights per half cycle. It was good to gather the male and female young to enjoy each other's company. They would not grow to maturity being strangers from their own.

Bahari didn't know why or when their society became this way. Once in every full cycle, he gathered with the other female and male breeders, in a chosen lagoon, surrounded by a beautiful reef. During these festivals, several lights of ritualistic underwater ceremonies took place. On these occasions, the comings of age males were introduced formally to their female counterparts. This was done, of course, under the close supervision of their breeding life givers. It was the time for each youth to seek out a breeding partner, one he or she would permanently bond with.

The Delmar, as a kind and loving society, took care of their youth. No young were forced to choose a mate. It had to develop naturally. When it failed to happen with a female or male, they were without question, comforted and taken back to their own intimate pod, until the next breeding cycle.

The Delmar lived, by tradition, in two separate pods. When either a male or female Delmar was born, he or she would be kept in their birth giver's arms for two full cycles. By that time, the new spawn would be ready to be taken from its birth givers' nourishment.

In the case of a female, at two cycles she becomes part of the matriarchal society, nurtured, taught and tenderly protected until she was grown enough to join in on the mating cycles. For the male youth, at two cycles, they were given over to their breeding male, to be raised and taught the ways of the undersea world. They too, when the proper cycle was reached, would be allowed to choose a breeding partner.

This process had to be carefully supervised by both, the male and female Elders. Living separately for so many cycles, the young had to be steered towards opposites who were not of their immediate lineage. All adult Delmar were taught the importance of diversity within the pod, to assure strength in their continuing lines.

It endangered the entire Delmar existence, whenever their movements were compromised. Often fast action was required to protect their entire community. Especially, when forced migrations happened in dangerous times. The necessary caring for Delmar, who were unable to keep up with the pod, caused ongoing concern. It was not in their nature to leave any behind, no matter how horrible the crisis.

Bahari loved these festivals and official play times. It gave him a rare chance to spend a full light, with his breeding partner. He loved the sight of Yahaira. Hovering in her arms was Varun, the male spawn they had produced last cycle. It would be another full cycle before Bahari would be required to take possession of his new tiny male. Meanwhile he let no occasion pass without spending as much time as possible with Yahaira at his side and Varun happily enfolded in his strong arms.

Best of all, at the time of the next cycle, Bahari will spend several lights in a special place. While there, he and Yahaira will continually bring their physical beings passionately together, in belief that a new life will soon be appearing.

Bahari's friend and nurturing partner Jennis suddenly let out a happy roar. Looking towards where Jennis was facing, the reason was obvious. Several of the almost of age males were hovering, in obvious embarrassment, behind a large outcropping of sea growth and rock. From where they hovered, both Bahari and Jennis could observe the reason.

Young Delmar males differed in this respect to their pillared counterparts. Being of almost breeding age, they developed a strong embarrassment at the thought of exposing their breeding members to the mixed gathering of Delmar youth. The young males had physically reacted, to being in close contact with the near reproductive aged females. Their breeding appendages had involuntarily and all too firmly, protruded from behind their protective folds.

Bahari and Jennis roared their happy sound in unison. Jennis's eldest, Gazsi, was among the young males, in a similar uncontrolled state. Jennis and Bahari well remembered those embarrassing times from their youth. Both knew that in no time, the young ones' obvious excitement would subside and they would re-join the youthful activities.

3

Looking in another direction, Jennis motioned for Bahari to observe. Two of the young males who were almost of age to mate could be seen. They were off together, in a secluded part of the lagoon. Keone and Nadish were swirling, embraced in an intimate arc of pleasurable motion. Bahari believed that by next full cycle, they would probably do as most and choose a breeding partner. Then, as was Delmar custom, they would return to the comfort and intimacy of each others arms, once the mating season was over. If they did not seek breeding mates, so be it. They did look sensuously excited and happy in each other's embrace.

Nearby his side, Yahaira was also watching the interaction between Keone and Nadish. She sounded to Bahari that both she and Keone's birth giver were so happy for their union of friendship.

Bahari wanted to know why especially their friendship? Should it be different than the one he shared with Jennis? Yahaira would not reveal more through sounds. She drew Bahari tighter to her side and sounded that if he observed closer he would know why their happiness was special.

Drifting a little lower, all of a sudden Bahari got a fast glimpse of what was happening. Keone and Nadish were swirling face to face in each other's arms. This was a favored pastime for all youth and their intimate partners.

What Bahari realized was amazing. Not surprisingly, in his passionate embrace, Keone's mating organ had escaped its protective folds. While it was obviously fully engorged, it was not the object of Nadish's attention. Bahari realized that Nadish was thrusting in copulation with Keone. But instead of entering him from behind as males did, he was thrusting into the folds just above Keone's exposed mating organ.

Turning to Yahaira Bahari asked if that was possible or was he imagining it? Yahaira sounded that it was the reason they made a perfect match. Keone obviously had both female and male organs within his folds. Nadish had discovered this in their early days as young Delmar males. They had grown and developed together. By the time they were old enough to interact intimately, Nadish soon learned to enjoy the pleasure of Keone's added feature.

Bahari sounded that because of his fast approaching reproductive cycle, it was obviously evident that while Keone had the entry part of a birth giver's channel, he didn't possess the inner workings that would allow him to conceive and create a new Delmar spawn.

Bahari, as all of his kind knew, the most important rule of the Delmar tradition was that all creatures deserved to live a happy and safe existence. This same belief encompassed not only them, but also all other creatures who shared their water world, as well as the dry world above.

Bahari had met Jennis in the first cycle, when he was taken to live with the males. Jennis was two cycles older. Bahari was smitten, from his first light, cradled in his breeder's arms. In this, his new world of male Delmar, he was instantly attracted to the robust activity that Jennis displayed. Observing this four-cycle-old spawn immediately became Bahari's main fascination.

They grew together and in time, as maturity blossomed, loved deeply. But once every full cycle, when the waters warmed in their mating festival place, they both happily drifted apart, seeking out their breeding partners.

Bahari was with Yahaira, the first partner that he became enthralled with, as a young breeding aged male. They had, over the cycles, produced three male and three female spawn.

Jennis, on the other hand, had only been with his youthful choice of breeding partner for just less than two cycles. Her sound was Marella. They had produced one male spawn. He had been given the sound, Gazsi. Barely more than one cycle after bringing forth their first male, Marella had been caught in the fury of a terrible raging surface. She was overcome by the surging water between a reef and the rocky dry place. Devastatingly, for both her and Jennis, she did not survive.

The following cycle, Jennis was fortunate enough to attract a new partner, Negeen. She had lost her breeding male, while attempting to reach safety during the same raging of the waters' surface. Tenderness quickly flourished. Being still young and extremely healthy, their physical needs quickly overrode their all too crushing grief. By early in the following tropical place cycle, they happily produced a new male spawn. They gave him the sound Galia.

Bahari sometimes wondered what it would be like, if their customs were different. If he could live in a way which a male remained with his female breeding partner always? He had no desire to challenge their tradition though. He treasured his time, both in the beautiful arms of his breeding partner Yahaira, and in the strong muscular arms of his male life partner, Jennis.

Like all Delmar society, Bahari accepted tradition. Some however, did not evolve to be attracted to their opposites. Be they male or female, their natural drives kept them totally committed to staying with their own for life. Bahari though, thoroughly enjoyed the sensual pleasures that the varied tradition afforded.

Yahaira was beautiful and voluptuous, with long flowing, shimmering golden hair. She had amazingly large, mounds on her chest. These had been the impetus that originally fueled Bahari's youthful passion for Yahaira. But during their first cycle together, he fell passionately for Yahaira herself. She was a loving creature; it soon grew to become much more. He had to accept the fact this sensuous feature of Yahaira's being was not exclusively for his pleasure. They also provided the nourishment, to grow their offspring, into a healthy and strong state.

One light, when Yahaira was feeding their tiny second-born Larina, they had an amazing and intimate encounter. Bahari had mistakenly passed near Yahaira's private feeding place. As was her right to do so, she had not sent him immediately away. That light she allowed Bahari to observe the little one, hungrily taking nourishment.

When tiny Larina's needs were satisfied, Yahaira motioned Bahari to come nearer. He will never forget that sensuous interlude. They could not mate, but they could passionately caress each other and cradle their newborn.

At one point during the encounter, reaching for the little one, Bahari's face brushed against Yahaira's swollen feeders. Rather than recoil, she drew him closer, guiding his strong lips to her feeding place. It had been so many cycles since Bahari had been a tiny spawn, he had forgotten how rich and warm a birth giver's nourishment tasted.

As he consumed the life giving nectar from Yahaira, he lost control, causing his now rigid breeding member to escape from its folds. Rather than rejecting him, Yahaira first pressed his hungry lips, firmly against her feeding place. She then reached down and comforted his painful shaft, until it gave forth with breeding fluid.

Once this happened, he was able to finally relax in her arms, while cradling Larina against his muscular chest. They parted later that light, in order to proceed to where they were expected to be. The gentle times as well as the sensuous times in Yahaira's arms were incredible. That light only served to fuel Bahari's love for Yahaira, to even deeper depths.

Later that dark, in the arms of Jennis, Bahari was insatiable in his lust. This was unlike their usual passionate darks. During most, Jennis dominated, leaving Bahari gasping in spent pleasure. This dark, Bahari ravaged Jennis, until he almost lost awareness.

Jennis was long, slim in his middle, strong and extremely muscular across his upper half. Being two cycles older than Bahari, he was generally much larger and stronger. His magnificent strength and form was an inherited gift from his life givers. Like Bahari, he had hair that glistened like the deepest dark. It flowed in thick splendor the length of his broad muscular back. Bahari found the sheer power and strength of being enveloped in his arms and completely possessed, incredibly fulfilling.

Jennis' life breeding partner Negeen, was larger in structure, than Yahaira. Her hair was the color of the flaming coral that flourished in the warm places. Like the coral, Negeen's flowing tresses brilliantly glowed, when bright light filtered through the shallow water's depth. Negeen was presently quite rounded, carrying Jennis's new spawn.

As breeding pairs, Negeen and Jennis, like Bahari and Yahaira, were so different in coloring from their partners. There was always a special excitement in waiting to see whether the new spawn would be male or female, plus also of what hair, flesh tone and eye coloring their wonderful new spawn would have.

4

Looking across the play lagoon, Bahari was happy to see Delja, a female of his birth cycle, who he knew well. She was hovering in intimate communication with her new breeding partner Zeeman. She had been emotionally devastated and lost, when her first life breeding partner Cephas, was mortally attacked, by a deep predator. He was, that light, anticipating his second mating festival with Delja; they had previously produced their first spawn, Trai, who had arrived so early that he was unable to survive.

Overwhelmed by a second crushing sorrow, Delja broke the most sacred rule of Delmar society. In her grief, she spurned the comfort that was generously offered from her community of female Delmar. She simply wanted to be alone, away from her kind. Without realizing where she was traveling, her grief took her dangerously towards the dry place.

Not far from the surf line, she spotted a beautiful young pillared male. He was uncovered from the middle up, obviously enjoying the warmth of the sun, as he quietly fished alone. He was being kept afloat by a strange small wooden craft.

In her grief and loneliness, Delja approached the male, and made herself known. Her whole being was shaking with terror. She knew that what she was doing was horribly wrong. Her blinding grief and desperation gave Delja the courage to risk all. She needed to be loved, to the point of disregarding everything that she had been taught.

The young pillared male was at first shocked, then intrigued by Delja's beauty. She looked like nothing that he had ever seen before. The simple mystery of her beautiful flowing hair and upper nakedness was overwhelming to his senses. It caused him to also throw caution, as well as the folk lore tales of death at the hands of 'Sea Sirens', aside.

Delja soon enchanted him into the waves. Making her sound for him, he realized what she meant. He responded with his sound, "Jasper". They played intimately together every light, for the entire warm cycle. He was as if at home, on the surface of her world. From that first light on, Jasper removed his entire covering before joining Delja upon the waves.

Delja loved the feeling of his flesh covered pillars as he entered her, wrapping them around her lower half. His pillars were long and his structure was slim, firm and only ever so slightly muscular. He was still just a youth, obviously several cycles younger than Delja.

His breeding appendage was enormous, compared to his slight size. In her grief-driven need, Delja could not get enough of him, filling her completely. It all too soon became evident. They had created a new spawn. Through their warm season together, Delja's belly continued to swell.

Delja's time to give forth a new life came sooner than expected. It should have happened only in thirty or forty more lights. By then she would have migrated with her pod to the warm place. That light, Delja was by Jasper's floating craft. He was nervous and afraid as he entered the warm water to comfort and assist her.

Unknown to Jasper, Delja's intention was to transport him and their tiny spawn to her world, deep below the waves. She knew that her lover could not survive in her realm, but she would have him resting close and his living Delmar spawn to remember him by.

Sadly for Delja, when she gave forth her new male spawn, was not a fully formed Delmar. He was like his breeding male Jasper. He had tiny flesh covered pillars. He also had flesh shaped openings on the sides of his head. There were no vents that would allow him to exist below the waves.

To take them to her realm, would have meant the end for both. The mothering instincts in her overrode Delja's emotions. Her little one could not be harmed.

She drew her newborn to her feeding place, cradling him as he took his first nourishment. When he had his fill, in tears, Delja gave him the sound, Ennis. She then lifted her tiny creature out of the waves, kissed him and placed him in the arms of her beautiful breeding male. Jasper was, by then, safely in his floating craft.

Delja was yet again, torn apart with loss. Flowing tears of grief, she watched as her pillared male lovingly wrapped their little one in the folds of his upper covering and lifting the large cloth to the top of its pillar, he let the wind carry him away.

To see Delja finally happy, cavorting with her new breeding male, was comforting. Zeeman was, thankfully, of her own kind. Seeing them together made every Delmar in the gathering smile. By the shape of Delja's slightly rounded belly, it was obvious. By next cycle there would be a new little one, one who could safely exist below the surface of the waves.

While Delja, was now feeling happy and fulfilled, in the arms of Zeeman, she still bore sadness in her heart. She could not forget her pillared lover, Jasper, and Ennis, her little male spawn

Later during that half cycle, Delja unexpectedly sought out Zeeman. Drawing him away from his activity, she led him towards the surface. She did not communicate her intentions that light and was acting strangely. Zeeman knew that he was not being led away for an intimate encounter. They had completed their first mating cycle a large number of lights ago. Both he and Delja were happy and confident. She was continually growing rounder. There was no denying it. Delja carried a new Delmar life in her belly.

As they neared the water's surface, Delja stopped her forward motion and scanned the horizon, obviously seeking something. She suddenly grabbed Zeeman's hand and drew him, upward and onward.

Zeeman was afraid, well knowing that they were breaking Delmar laws. He was especially alarmed as Delja urged him closer to the surf line. They soon approached a small floating structure. This was totally against their rules.

Breaching the surface, Zeeman could see a young pillared male. He was balancing upright, holding onto a sturdy pillar of wood. It pointed towards the ski sprouting from the center of his craft. Shockingly for Zeeman he was totally uncovered. Zeeman held back, unsure. He had never before been face to face with a live pillared creature. He had certainly never seen one of them in its entirety, upright, uncovered and dry.

Seeing Delja with Zeeman at her side, Jasper also hesitated. He was unsure; was he now in danger as folk lore suggested? Sensing his uncertainty, Delja smiled, making his sound and motioned him forward. His love for her gave him the courage and strength, to slide over the edge of his craft into her world.

Delja immediately enveloped him in an intimate embrace. While being held in Delja's arms, the young pillared male Jasper looked questioningly towards Zeeman.

Delja motioned him closer, opening one arm, to envelope Zeeman. Her pillared partner Jasper, was tense at first, but in no time relaxed. Both Delja and Zeeman smiled at each other, when they became aware of the pillared male's breeding member. It was involuntarily pressing into their intimate grouping. Delja, now being held tightly in the arms of her two males, was ecstatically happy. She placed a hand on each lover's chest. She then made their sounds, so that they would know each other.

It was natural for Delja and Zeeman to hover at the surface, with only a minimum of flexing. Embracing Jasper tightly in their arms, allowed him to stay afloat without exertion.

For the longest while Delja took care to direct each male, to explore the differences in their structures. Starting at the top, Zeeman was amazed, running his fingers through and feeling that Jasper's hair had been obviously made short. It barely reached half way to his shoulders. The concept of removing or shortening hair was not part of the Delmar's culture. He was fascinated; examining the flesh shapes that protruded from the sides of Jasper's head. Likewise, Jasper, after running his hands in amazement through the long strands of Zeeman's hair was all but afraid to touch Zeeman's vents. Realizing this, Zeeman turned his head and flexed his vents so that Jasper could observe how they worked.

Zeeman also found it curiously strange, that Jasper had a sparse growth of hair, on his upper front. He ran his hands along Jasper's chest, following the slight hair pattern downwards. While Zeeman did this, Jasper's hands explored the amazingly massive and firm muscled form of Zeeman's upper half.

When Zeeman's wandering hands reached Jasper's lower half, he reached for and embraced his engorged breeding member. Realizing that it was Zeeman not Delja who was now firmly grasping his manhood, Jasper recoiled slightly.

Neither Zeeman nor Delja could be aware of the reality of Jasper's culture. The society of Pillared males generally lived by a different code of conduct from the Delmar. By tradition, for the most part, their males existed separately, devoid of intimate physical relationships. They could not know that in the pillared society there were occasional exceptions. Like the Delmar, pillared ones at times are drawn to be exclusively with their own, be it male or female.

Looking deep into Delja's eyes, her land lover Jasper smiled and soon relaxed. To help make him understand their true similarities, she reached into Zeeman's folds and drew out his now fully hardened breeding member. She took her land lover's hand, gently placing it on Zeeman's member. Now she was truly happy; they were all as one.

Being so firmly pressed together, her pillared lover sensed the slight change in Delja's form. He ran his free hand over her middle, questioningly. Realizing what he meant, Delja placed her hand on her Delmar lover's chest. She then placed it on her slightly swollen middle. Jasper smiled, realizing that Delja was now as she should be, being reproductive with her own kind.

Suddenly Delja heard a sound, sensing a movement in the floating craft. Her pillared lover broke from their embrace and reached into the craft.

To Delja's total joy, he drew out their sleepy, one cycle old male, Ennis. Removing his coverings, he lowered their spawn into the waves, while taking care to keep his head above the surface. Delja wept with love and happiness, as she cradled Ennis in her arms. In unison the three closed in to make an intimate gathering, bouncing and playing with the little pillared male. He was obviously like his breeding male. He truly loved being immersed in the warm water. As they floated him back and forth in the protective circle, he squealed with joy.

That was when Delja made a wonderful discovery. As Ennis made his little one sounds, he suddenly became clear in communicating with Delja. In response she communicated with Ennis, using her traditional Delmar sounds and vibrations. Ennis smiled, making motions and deep inner vibrations, according to Delja's commands. Her happiness was now complete. While not being able to live below the waves with her, Ennis could at least learn to fully communicate, using her sounds and the vibrations of the deep. This surprising development was immediately also realized by Zeeman. In short order, observing the actions and hearing a great many but not all of the sounds, Jasper also shockingly realized what was happening.

The intimate gathering lasted for quite a while. Delja all too soon became aware, that her infant pillared spawn, was starting to shiver and shake. She knew the inevitable. Her world below the waves was not his natural environment, nor could it ever be. It was time to cover him up for warmth and return him to the floating craft.

Placing him aboard, seeing that Delja was in tears, her lover Jasper turned and passionately embraced both her and Zeeman. Then he climbed back aboard his little craft. His first action was to replace the coverings on Ennis's form, to keep him warm and protected.

This pleased Delja. Jasper was all that she had hoped for, a loving, nurturing and caring pillared male. He then placed a covering over his lower half, leaving his upper half exposed to the bright heat. Jasper then pulled on the cord bringing the heavy weight aboard that was maintaining his craft's position. He hauled on another cord and raised the soft billowing mass, to the top of its shaft. As it filled with air, the wind carried it forward and they started for the shore.

As they moved off into the distance, Jasper motioned to Delja, pointing to himself, then to little Ennis, lovingly cradled in his arms and finally to the water's surface, where she and Zeeman still hovered.

As only a mother could know, Delja knew that each full cycle during these lights, her pillared lover would return as often as possible with their spawn, so that she could lovingly hold Ennis. She was happy to know and observe his growth. Now thanks to her amazing discovery, she would also look forward to communicating fully with him. Delja was instantly excited in anticipation, foreseeing that by next full cycle, she would be able to present her new Delmar spawn, to Jasper and their little pillared male, Ennis.

28   Nino Balistreri

5

This was an in between cycle, when Bahari's breeding partner, Yahaira, was still nursing their tiny male spawn, Varun. Therefore he could not mate, to give her a new life. He wanted in its place, to make a gift to Yahaira, to show his ongoing love. Several lights before, he had gone to a special, extremely deep place, that he and Jennis had found. As youthful spawn they loved to explore together and discover.

The remains of a large old wooden surface craft lay broken deep below on the rock strewn bottom. It was well on its way to being dissolved by the tiny burrowing sea creatures. They formed the foundation of life below the waves. In the midst of the wreckage, Bahari and Jennis had found a burst container. It was filled with beautiful things.

Over the cycles, as the large craft dissolved, more became evident. Much of the craft and its contents had corroded and all but disappeared in the swirling currents. But the shiny items kept their beauty. Bahari and Jennis had learned as youth that while it was safe to explore these sunken craft, it was not safe to delve into or alter them in order to explore deeply. The burrowing creatures and time took care of it all. As the cycles came and went, more and more of the shiny contents came within easy reach.

Each new cycle, Bahari and Jennis knew to approach the craft with caution. They had observed many times before when the pillared ones used special coverings and mechanisms to find these sites and extract the shiny things. Luckily, this craft was so deep and hidden among giant boulders, it had never been discovered. Jennis and Bahari knew that the cycle might come when they would find it stripped of all it possessed. This was an accepted fact in the Delmar world. Thankfully for them at least, there were other places and many other sunken craft to explore.

Hovering above the debris, Bahari selected a flexible circle of ornate metal. He was unsure why this shiny material did not dissolve, like much of the rest that was part of the craft. He was just pleased that it remained flexible and brilliant. Suspended from the circle, it had a solid mass of similar ornate metal. This was embedded with beautiful colored stones. They were brilliant, like the tiny creatures that populated the reef, surrounding their warm place. But unlike the small living creatures, these stones were hard and quite translucent.

He knew that Yahaira would be pleased with this offering. He so wished that she would allow him to mate with her, just for pleasure today. He full well knew, she could not physically conceive, not until the light arrived, when their tiny Varun had reached two cycles. But he loved Yahaira so. His desire levels had risen at the sight of her. He needed to feel the sheer ecstasy of being as one, locked in her folds.

Unfortunately he knew from life's experience, Yahaira would not feel in any way, the need for this physical bonding. She was always intimately close, when they spent lights together. But it was strangely bred into female Delmar., that they had no desire for physical coupling, until they were in their conceiving cycle.

Unlike Delmar females, the males were driven from an early age with the constant need to have fulfilled relief. Thankfully the males had their life partners, to satisfy their lust driven passion. The ache in Bahari's breeding area was intense. When this play time was over, he and Jennis would returned to their own special resting place. This dark, Jennis would need to take all of the fury of Bahari's pent up passion. Bahari's need was too intense. This dark he must dominate their union with all of his frustrated, bursting virility. Only when he is fully spent, would he finally succumb, letting Jennis totally possess him.

Being so near Yahaira and his little male spawn, it was taking all of Bahari's mature strength, to not burst forth. Like the young males, allowing his ample and now painful breeding member to embarrassingly escape from its protective folds. Bahari was proud of his breeding appendage. His life partner Jennis, while being larger and more muscular, had a slightly shorter and much thinner member. Bahari was pleased with this, because Jennis was highly driven. He needed to possess Bahari completely, often multiple times every dark. When the role was reversed on occasion, Bahari knew that Jennis suffered from the near brutal use of his larger member. But Jennis loved Bahari so dearly, he gladly endured.

Together they cared for and taught the collection of both their male offspring. In Delmar society, the males as well as the females separately raised their ever growing spawn. Having a special partner like Jennis helped to ensure their own young, were kept safely away from danger and educated carefully.

There certainly was no division between the male and female Delmar when it came to tenderness and nurturing skills. The main difference in their societal makeup was developed by need and security. Both male and female Delmar raised and nurtured their spawn. But for the preservation and safety of all Delmar existence, the male population had to be raised with the skills to protect and defend. Often their numbers were bolstered by unattached strong female Delmar. But as a rule their strength and skills were well used as a second defense, to care for the safety of the female and infant members of the pod.

6

Life beneath the waves was enjoyable, but at the same time extremely dangerous. Raging waters, surface craft with their massive woven fibers trailing, pillared creatures, as well as the occasional sea creature, posed an ongoing danger to the Delmar's existence.

Surprisingly, many creatures that they shared their world with, could and did at times turn on the Delmar. All too often, even they lost the ability to comprehend that the Delmar were in no way a threat to their existence. It was a dangerous undertaking. When a sea creature lost control and attacked, the Delmar males had no choice, but to band together, overcome their natural revulsion to aggression and destroy the threat.

Early the next light, Bahari and Jennis gathered their spawn in a special place. They had chosen it, for education. It helped their male offspring to know that this was not a play place. The older two were well motivated in their gathering of food, knowledge and sounds. The graduating cycles of younger Delmar males had to continually learn as their abilities developed. By the cycle they became of age, they had to be proficient in food gathering and knowledge of their world of waters and both its pleasures and dangers. This knowledge was vital to their continued safety and actual existence.

The Delmar had learned from generations past, to communicate using gestures, as well as deep from within, vibrating tones. These sounds were not unlike those of the air breathing sea creatures. The only actual sounds that they vocalized were learned from the pillared creatures. That's where their society formed the recognition of their individual identities.

They had no practical need for a litany of vocalizations, but it was tradition. When a new spawn was presented to the community of Delmar Elders, it was custom. On these special occasions, the breeding life-givers had to choose a pillared creature's sound. These strange titles for their beings were an ever expanding learning curve, for the Delmar society.

When a Delmar was accidentally seen peering above the surface, a pillared creature would always call out, usually in a different strange way, depending where they were spotted. Every Delmar was tasked to listen carefully to these sounds and report them back to the Elders, especially if the sound was new, one that had not yet been learned.

These strange vocalizations became individual titles, for future generations of spawn to accept. No Delmar elders could explain why the pillared creatures did not call them by one sound.

They only had limited accepted sounds for them, 'Pillared Creatures' or 'Pillared ones'. Sometimes but rarely, they titled them, 'Flesh creatures', because of their total flesh covering.

When a surface craft floundered and sank beneath the waves, it was a chance for the education of the older youth, while conveying the many distressed creatures to the safety of their dry place or the lifeless ones to their resting place. On these occasions, each breeding male was able to pass on knowledge to his older spawn. Invariably, in every group of pillared creatures who perished beneath the waves, it was the same. There were always a number of them who wore no covering at the time of their craft floundering. In some instances it was obvious that the raging waters had torn most of the coverings free from their beings.

It was taught to the youth over cycles. These creatures were in many ways like the Delmar. On close examination, they had similar eye and mouth openings as well as arms and hands. They also had similar breeding appendages. The most dramatic difference lay on the sides of their heads and the bottom half of their structures.

The pillared people were considered by the Delmar, to be of inferior design. They had no means of extracting life sustenance; by ingesting the ocean's fluid and filtering out its rich nutrients. They were also incapable of extracting the necessary gasses from the water. This process was essential for the preservation of life below the waves, just as in drawing in the air above was essential to maintain life for all dry place creatures.

The Delmar did have the ability to sustain life with their heads above the waves, as well as in their natural environment below the surface. Certainly the Delmar recognized that long term exposure to the dry atmosphere above did cause severe discomfort, especially in the area of their vents.

The land creatures had one additional major failing that was well recognized by the Delmar. Their flesh had no long term resistance to the water. Once immersed, it became soft, quickly deteriorating. This was especially so if life had left their being. The Delmar's upper half, although covered with flesh, had a much firmer consistency. Unlike the land creatures, it was not affected by immersion below the waves.

The worst feature that the dry creatures were perceived to have, was that both the females and males of their species had not developed a natural protection for their breeding areas. The males looked strange, with their members hanging vulnerably out. It was generally agreed by the Delmar. Because their breeding areas were dangerously exposed, it caused the pillared creatures to wear the varied coverings, to protect themselves from both embarrassment and injury.

7

Several darks later, the light dawned, in a much deeper tone than usual. The natural flow of current felt strangely disturbed. It alternated between almost still calm and sudden rushing. As on all similar occasions, the Elders quickly sent forth a decree. All of the Delmar must gather their spawn and cherished ones, then proceed to a deeper safer place, a one that tradition had set aside for these dangerous times.

Later, as Bahari and Jennis settled to rest, closely encircling their spawn for safety, they could feel it begin. No Delmar had to surge towards the surface, in order to observe what was happening. To do so would have invited danger, and as they all knew, the real possibility of death. It was common Delmar experience, learned from Elder to birth givers. The waters above were wildly raging. The only safety lay in remaining deep and gathered tightly in the comfort of each other's warm embrace. The raging of the waters grew and grew as the dark lingered on. It seemed that there would be no limit to the horrors of the waters through that entire dark.

The tortured surface continued to roar on, for two lights and three dark's. This was indeed a bad upheaval of the waters surface. Normally these violent events had ended by this point in the cycle. But all Delmar knew that the waters and the air above went by its own plan. It was calm and warm or cold and wild with no real set schedule. Every time the Delmar assumed that it would be one way or the other, it shocked and surprised them. The Elders believed that if they could only learn to predict these changes, they could better protect all those in their care.

When the churning waters finally settled, the Elders gave forth a signal. All Delmar could now return to their shallower places of rest. On the way upward to their usual resting place, Bahari and Jennis observed their surroundings. Several of the pillars in the festival area, had collapsed. But thankfully the wall and the arches remained. It would have been sad to lose it all. The youth so enjoyed their play time in the unusual currents.

Once their spawn were settled and safe, Bahari and Jennis took turns. Bahari took Dylon at his side and Jennis took his eldest Gazsi. This was an important lesson for their fast maturing spawn to learn. It was a crucial task, for the safety of all Delmar creatures. On these occasions, the adults and older spawn must explore their surrounding rest and feeding places, to observe what the raging waters had done. The entire exercise was to maintain security, for the safety of the younger as well as weaker members of their kind.

Not far from their resting place, Jennis found a surface craft lying on the sandy bottom. This craft had not been seen before. It wasn't an overly large one, just long and slim. By touching it Jennis could tell, it was not made of wood, but of some type of extremely smooth and bright material.

Jennis and Gazsi explored around the craft. They found many strange articles that were strewn in an arch on the sandy bottom. But thankfully this time, there were no pillared creatures needing to be laid to rest. He assumed that they had either been rescued by a larger craft, or were swept away with the raging currents, far beyond this immediate place.

As decreed by tradition, Jennis reported his find to the Elders. It was their duty to examine the craft. Once fully explored, they would decree if it was safe, to let the youth play around and on it. If they so decreed that it was not safe, no Delmar would go near it. The Elders knew what was best to protect all members of the pod.

By next light, the decree was announced through the Delmar community. The more sensitive of the Elders could perceive a pulse, emanating from the craft. They knew that when this happened, pillared creatures often followed this pulse, allowing them to investigate and often raise the sunken craft. Because of this, it was not safe to be discovered in the area. They commanded all the Delmar, to temporarily move their resting places, well away from the sunken craft.

A hidden watch was set up to observe the craft. After only four lights, a surface craft was detected. It sent a weight crashing to the ocean floor, with a long line attached. As the Delmar had observed, many times before, several pillared creatures soon entered the water. They were covered in a fitted dark substance, unlike their usual flesh covering. The Delmar believed that these coverings were designed to protect their weak flesh from the effects of immersion. They also wore a clear apparatus that covered their eyes, as well as their mouth.

Fin type appendages, not part of their natural being, were attached to the ends of their supporting pillars. It provided them with the propulsion, to surge forward. These appeared to be designed to perform, much like the Delmar used their fan like appendages. Each creature also carried large shining tubular shapes strapped to their backs.

It did not take long. They went directly to the craft, somehow drawn by the signal it emitted. The creatures spent some time swarming all around the stricken craft. One of the watchers observed two of the creatures being signaled by the third. He had just emerged from within the opening, on the top of the craft. The pillared creature could be seen shaking his head then pointing towards the surface. It was taken that they would do nothing, towards recovering the craft. To be completely safe, the Elders kept the entire community away from that area for several more lights.

When no other craft or pillared creatures approached, they decreed that the area was now safe. Because of the floating cords and billowing shrouds, hanging from its two thin columns, it was also decreed that the youth were not to be allowed to play around this craft. In all times past, small sea creatures quickly went to work, consuming these soft trailing substances, as well as the actual structure of the craft. But in more recent cycles, the billowing folds of texture and trailing lines, along with the crafts themselves were of a strange consistency. It all seemed to be of a substance that the burrowing creatures could not digest.

8

Bahari and Jennis had their male spawn to jointly care for and teach. The youngest two were just three cycles old. Jennis's little spawn's sound was Galia. Bahari's had been given the sound, Zamar. They had now been with Bahari & Jennis for one full cycle and were still adjusting to being fully with the male society. By next full cycle, Bahari's Varun and Jennis's Shui would replace Zamar and Galia, as being the youngest spawn in their intimate pod.

At least once, in every four or five lights, they altered their routine. Rather than leading the spawn as an entire group, to explore their surroundings and learn. Bahari and Jennis divided them up. They took the youngest two away from their older siblings. Doing this helped to keep the older spawn focused on absorbing information. The little spawn's third and forth cycles with the males, were the most important ones. Being absorbed into their new grouping just as they entered their third cycle, they learned quickly.

As a complete group of all cycles, it was a natural happening. The little one's short attention span worked against them. It caused them to mostly watch the elder spawn. The elder youth loved to put on a show for the little ones, portraying it all their activities as a game, while each robustly flowed through their daily routines.

The more mature spawn knew what water growth was safe to consume, as well as where it was safe to play and gather their varied nourishment needs. Their youngest two had still much to be taught. Part of every light was devoted to education. On these special times, the lessons were separately geared to the level of maturity. Bahari and Jennis had learned well. They knew that the individual groups and cycles of spawn, absorbed knowledge and achieved at different rates.

Bahari and Jennis also had one spawn each, at the older end of the scale. Jennis had Gazsi. He was just one full cycle away from being accepted into the mating phase of his development. Gazsi was much like his father, strong and large in build. He like Jennis had long flowing hair. Unlike Jennis's extremely dark mane, Gazsi's was caught, between fair and dark. This was a beautiful gift of remembrance, from his birth giver Marella, who was no longer with them.

Like Jennis, he also had the confidence to openly exhibit his abilities. He loved nothing better than to perform feats of maneuvering and strength, especially whenever he was alone with the younger spawn, as audience. It was always a constant task to keep the spawn safe, while at the same time allowing them the freedom to explore and learn.

Just two lights past, Jennis and Bahari had cause to be upset with both their eldest spawn. That mid light when it was time to have a short rest, the spawn had all gone as a group, to their favorite comfort place. Rather than join them there, as they often did, this light, Bahari and Jennis decided to spend some intimate time, resting in each other's arms. Waking after a while, Jennis and Bahari sleepily drifted over to rejoin their spawn. This light, they were not as usual, all gathered in one intimate mass, asleep in each other's arms.

Cautiously approaching, Bahari and Jennis could see a gathering. Their spawn, along with several others, were all awake and hovering in a semi circle. Their eldest, Gazsi and Dylon, hovered at the head of the group. They had obviously taken on the lead, to show the younger spawn how their bodies' development worked.

Gazsi was hovering in all his massive glory, with muscles fully flexed. Bahari and Jennis settled behind a large growth of fern, to observe where this demonstration was leading. Just as they expected, as dictated by his nature, Gazsi was the prime exhibit. He floated proudly in front of the gathering of young spawn, while Dylon carefully instructed them. Dylon was bringing attention to every area, of the strength and shapes of Gazsi's magnificent muscular structure.

As the instruction worked its way down, Bahari and Jennis had to shift a little, to see why all of the young spawn had so intently leaned forward, in order to get a better view. Sure enough, the elder male youths were doing what they knew was wrong. But at the same time, it was a coming of age that traditionally happened, in one form or another. A smiling Gazsi was hovering, with his large and now excited breeding appendage in full view. Dylon was playing the instructor, explaining and showing the young spawn, every inch of Gazsi's engorged endowment.

Just as Bahari and Jennis were about to surge forward, to break up the gathering, they observed a shift in Gazsi. The expression on his face drastically changed. Looking closer it was obvious why. Dylon had stopped pointing out Gazsi's features. He had now taken Gazsi's large breeding member in hand. Before they could be reached and stopped, Dylon's handling brought Gazsi to an explosive conclusion. Dylon then immediately swirled his hands through the thick liquid. Gathering it up he showed the breeding fluid around the circle, obviously explaining its purpose.

Neither Bahari nor Jennis had ever dealt with this situation before. Recovering from the shock of the display, they sent out signal sounds that they were approaching. Sensing this, the 'Learning circle', immediately broke up. Dylon could be seen herding the young spawn back to their resting place while urging the other immature male spawn to quickly return to the safety of their caregivers.

Meanwhile Gazsi was desperately struggling, as he turned in circles. He was painfully trying to envelope his still swollen appendage, back into its protective folds.

Jennis and Bahari resumed the day's activities, not letting on that they had witnessed the impromptu reproductive instructions. They knew that it would not be healthy if the younger spawn were in any way punished. Doing so would cause them to believe that the normal growth function of their body and reproductive organs was bad.

Later that light, Jennis and Bahari had the opportunity to take Dylon and Gazsi aside. Both males were chastised for teaching the all too young about their physical structure's development.

Dylon and Gazsi learned an important lesson that light. Their functions and intimate interaction with each other was completely acceptable to Bahari and Jennis. But there was a cycle when the young were ready to learn of these physical and emotional abilities. While they were still immature spawn, was not the advised cycle.

Jennis reminded their young males that he and Bahari had fully instructed them on the workings of their structure and organs, but only as it became appropriate. This was during the cycle that each in turn started to lose control. It was when each growing male experienced their organs uncontrollably bursting from their folds, first in simple rigid stubbornness, then later, as they matured, when their members began to randomly eject thick fluid. It was then, that the knowledge of what the thick fluid was for could be taught. Only then, they were mature enough to fully understand.

As they grew from tiny spawn and developed, it was totally acceptable for a young growing male to burst forth many times a light, with or without a fluid discharge. It just made their intimate play times all the more pleasurable in sensations, especially once they had formed a lasting bond with a life partner.

From early on, Delmar males and females were taught to accept their growing appendages with natural interest. They were also encouraged to explore their sensations, along with the tactile feeling of their entire being. Later as their male mating structures approached full growth, it tended to often happen, at all the wrong times. Then it became an embarrassing experience for the older male youth to endure.

At this point in their cycles of growth, being fully informed on what was happening, helped the young Delmar males to live with and somewhat control their physical functions.

9

Both Jennis and Bahari had for many cycles been aware that Gazsi was the dominant of their two eldest spawn. Following in Jennis's path, he was totally possessing Dylon, the passive member of their relationship. On first discovering this, Bahari had reported his finding to Jennis. Both were pleased that their fast maturing spawn had chosen each other to be life mates and protectors.

A young Delmar spawn, be they female or male, often learned this lesson the painful way. It was safer and more nurturing of love, to have a special life partner, to intimately develop and grow with. For a youth to wander without close companionship through the greater Delmar pod, looking for satisfaction and relief, was not good. Nor did it make their life safe.

This became even more evident, when they reached their time to accept the total responsibility of birthing and or nurturing their spawn. An intimate partnership increased both comfort and safety for the pair as well as the entire pod of Delmar.

The next full cycle would all too soon come around. Jennis observed what was now happening at every gathering. Gazsi had no shyness. He was already making intense, piercing eye contact, with several of the female youth. He was, totally possessed each light, when there was a festival or play time. His activity and speed kept both Bahari and Jennis in a whirl trying to monitor his behavior. They worried that his dominant strengths would carry over from his relationship with Dylon. If he displayed this before it was time, there would be trouble with the Elders and the breeding life givers of the female population.

Bahari's Dylon still had almost three cycles to mature, before he would be able to mate. He was still, physically unaffected by close contact with the young females. On play and festival days, Dylon could be observed hovering aside, with a questioning look on his face. The reason was obvious. He was observing this new strange behavior, as Gazsi surged around, showing off his prowess. For Dylon, watching Gazsi flexing his strong muscles, while interacting with the young females, was truly a strange sight. It was an attitude that he did not fully understand.

Dylon certainly knew about mating and the process that was involved in creating a new life. But because he still had not gained the drive to do so, he found Gazsi's attitude and activities quite unusual and alarming, not to mention the most obvious fact. While Gazsi was surging around impressing the many young female Delmar, he was, for the first time in his life, totally ignoring Dylon.

But Bahari and Jennis knew that just one to two more cycles would add the drive to mate to Dylon's existence.

Their older spawn were proving to be an ongoing concern. They took as much watching and guarding as the little ones, if not more. Daily, their confidence grew. It was one thing to be brave enough to orchestrate that show and tell demonstration, for the not fully mature spawn. It was another, to rocket off alone, exploring. More often than not, all the older youth did this, with little or no understanding of unknown areas, or regard for safety. Certainly Bahari and Jennis had enjoyed many adventures exploring as maturing spawn. One of these adventures had produced their special deep place for gathering the shiny gifts they gave.

Like many of the stronger and more virile young adult Delmar, Gazsi and Dylon believed themselves to be all powerful and immune to damage. Testing the limits of danger was an ever growing game for them. Jennis knew that once Gazsi chose a mating partner and fostered a new life, he would settle and become more responsible.

Gazsi would then quickly realize the importance of his situation. If he and his new breeding partner create a male spawn, his life will change more drastically. In just two cycles, his position as the breeding male would then become real. It would require him to bear the full responsibility of physically protecting and caring for his spawn. He would also be required to take on the gathering of safe foods, as well as the education of his little male.

Thinking about the all too soon approaching festival, in which Gazsi would become officially of breeding age, Bahari and Jennis made a decision. Each time one of their male spawn neared this important coming of age, they would go to the special place and retrieve a bright piece of treasure. They would give the gleaming article to their coming-of-age male spawn. He can then present it to his new mating partner. This would make a perfect bonding gift to begin their first intimate reproductive experience.

Likewise, as their female spawn came of age, Bahari and Jennis planned to do the same. But they decided that their female spawn would appreciate and cherish the shiny gift more, if it came from their newly chosen male mate. Bahari and Jennis would give the gifts to the intended male, so that he can proudly present it to his soon-to-mate female spawn. In both cases it would be a starting of life-cycle gift, for the new breeding pairs.

None of the young had ever been to the special mating lagoon. It was secluded, totally ringed by a reef. This lagoon was treasured, purposely excluded from their lives. The first time either a male or female Delmar experienced these beautiful depths, was always amazing. Exploring it and choosing a special place would enhance the young pair's soon to happen, erotic experience. They would hopefully come away from this intimate time with a forever breeding mate.

Leading up to the festival, Jennis, as the breeding life giver, would guide Gazsi around the nearby secret lagoon. It was tradition, to help him to choose a private place, within its multi-chambered depths, because it will be there, that he would first explore the wonders of intimacy with his new-found life choice.

10

Several lights later the new brightness barely awakened. It was both unsettled and dark. The elders, as always, instructed the Delmar to act quickly. On these occasions, they must take their young to the safe places, much deeper below the waves. During the following dark, the elders sounded the alarm.

A large pillared one's craft had floundered, on the wildly churning surface. The Delmar males, who were assigned for rescues, immediately went forth to observe. The reef was just a short distance from the dry place where the pillared creatures resided. They were obviously attempting to gain the safety of their protective cove, when the raging air and water drove their craft against the jagged rocks. There could be a need to save many.

In the case of Jennis and Bahari, because of their large number of young spawn needing protection, it was pre arranged. Jennis was designated to go forth with his exceptional strength, to give assistance to the desperate pillared creatures. Bahari was to stay behind, to protect their spawn. He would be called forth, only if a severe crisis occurred.

As the Delmar rescuers approached the raging surface, it was obvious. The stricken craft was breaking up against a reef, all too quickly sinking below the waves. Many of the pillared creatures were safely aboard small wooden craft. These were being discharged from the larger fast floundering craft. But a great number of others were in the water, crying out in extreme distress.

Being well versed in how to proceed, the Delmar males went into action. Using the raging waves as protection, reaching from below, they propelled the creatures towards the safety of their dry place. Once they were close to the surf line, they were each, in turn, released atop a giant swell. The dry place creatures had to be on their own, to struggle through the tumbling and raging surf, to their place of refuge.

Fully knowing that many would not survive this thundering torrent, the Delmar could do nothing to help them here. Doing so would heighten their chance of being discovered. It would have also greatly endangered them physically. With their entire existence spent beneath the surface of the great waters expanse, the Delmar truly understood the full fury of the raging waters. They could only survive it when they had great depths below to escape to.

Jennis was unaware that disaster would happen. Gazsi had left the protection of the deep and followed Jennis up to the raging surface. Observing what the other males were doing, he quickly maneuvered below a pillared creature and did the same. But for a good reason, this technique was only taught to the Delmar males, once they truly became adults.

Feeling strong and important, Gazsi failed to watch the other males closely. He did not realize in detail, how the adult males were carefully propelling the creatures. Each Delmar supported a chosen one atop a swell, to allow it to appear, that the powerful surf was carrying them forth to safety.

Gazsi was now surging forward, towards the dry place. He had chosen a male pillared creature to rescue. In his lack of knowledge, he had maneuvered dangerously close into the shallows where the surf crashed upon the dry place. Without warning, Gazsi found himself hurled free from the water's safety by the enormous surf. He was then violently slammed down against the rock-strewn bottom. This happened three times, before the raging vortex disappeared from his awareness and vision.

The next that Gazsi was barely aware of, he was in the arms of Jennis, being quickly propelled towards the deep and safety. Arriving at their resting place, in a total panic, Jennis roared the distress sound. This immediately brought Elder males and females to his side.

Gazsi was bruised and battered. His flesh was torn in many places and he was writhing in horrible pain. He was trying to pass a large enough volume of water through his vents. To fail to do so properly would all too soon cause death for a Delmar creature.

The head of the Elders, who had the sound Kye, was soon at their side. Kye was proficient in healing powers. He began to administer to Gazsi. He used a thick sticky substance gathered from a special sea creature. Carefully applying this substance, he was able to close and secure the tears in Gazsi's flesh. This stopped the loss of blood, helping to stabilize him. At the same time, it ensured that no predators in the area could become aware of the existence of distress triggered by the scent of blood flowing freely in the current.

To keep the damaged flesh secure, he then wrapped Gazsi's torn and battered chest and arms in an unusual long flat sea growth. Finally he wrapped his scraped and damaged scaly lower half in the same growth. Once this was complete, Kye rushed to his resting place. He quickly returned, with bits of a minute sea creature and a small piece of bright-colored sea growth.

He coached a now gasping and totally delirious Gazsi to consume both. Gazsi was in such shock, it was beyond him to object or question what he was being fed. Almost immediately, his entire form relaxed. He began at last to flow life sustaining water through his vents in a more natural way. This achieved, he quickly fell into a calm sleep. Kye hovered by Gazsi's side. He administered to his needs for many darks and lights.

Several times during each light and dark, Gazsi would stir, attempting to become aware. Each time, Kye immediately fed him the strange combination, causing him to again quickly settle.

Jennis was in crisis, because Gazsi was never totally responsive or aware. He just lay there as in a living death. Kye assured him that it was for a reason. He made Jennis understand, that if Gazsi was to survive his injuries, he needed to completely rest and heal slowly. If he woke and moved, as a strong youth his age would try to do, it would destroy the healing process and endanger his very existence.

During this time, Jennis's breeding mate Negeen was often at his side. Gazsi was not her own spawn, but she loved Jennis and wanted to comfort and support him in his time of despair. Each light she went about gathering for Kye both nourishment for himself as well as fulfilling his special needs to continue caring for Gazsi. Also hovering nearby, Dylon was closely following Jennis. He needed constant reassurance that his beloved Gazsi was out of danger.

After eight lights, the healer began to let Gazsi become more alert each time, before ingesting the restorative compound. Gazsi was obviously still in severe pain. Kye assured Jennis that he hoped the crisis was over. Gazsi's chest, back, arms and sides were badly discolored from being crushed against the rocky bottom.

The tears in his flesh were slowly bonding. It was evident that some of the more severe damages would leave behind many permanent marks as a reminder of his near death experience.

There were areas on his scaly lower half that had been torn clean. It was many lights before he could fully tolerate the pain. Having the healing sea growth wrappings removed for even short periods of time caused Gazsi obvious distress.

At last, after what seemed to Jennis, too many lights, there was clear evidence. Gazsi's flesh around his healing wounds was gaining its natural color. A fine covering of immature scales, were now filling in the torn and damaged areas on his lower half. It took the balance of the warm cycle, before Gazsi was well enough to once again rest through a dark with Dylon nestled in his arms.

During these lights and darks Kye was never far away. He checked on and administered to Gazsi several times during every light. As he healed and gained in strength, Gazsi started to feel embarrassed by the constant attention. Kye assured him that it was natural to want to be independent again. But Gazsi had to agree that Kye knew best what he needed. After all, he was truly grateful to Jennis for rescuing him and to Kye for saving his life.

In time the waters cooled, causing the Delmar to migrate to their tropical lagoons for the dark season. Gazsi was finally able to weakly propel on his own. But he could only do so, with Dylon at his side, gently assisting him with forward thrust. He could hover and move about carefully now, with minimal distress. But the exertion of prolonged thrust was beyond his current endurance levels.

To observe them gliding along with the pod served as a perfect example for all Delmar to see. It was evident how important having a life partner was. A lone male or female needing help would certainly be cared for by the entire pod. But having special loving help, in a time of need, definitely assisted the healing process.

Slowly but surely, Gazsi strengthened. He was by now much thinner. He looked more like an extended version of Dylon. A grateful Jennis was assured by Kye the Elder healer, that Gazsi was now well. In no time he should strengthen as before the accident and fill out to his natural thick robust form.

One light shortly after settling in their warm place, Dylan sought out Jennis alone. He confessed that Gazsi wanted to possess him once more. He was more than willing. He had desperately missed this aspect of their intimacy. But he was worried that it would be harmful and set Gazsi back in his recovery.

Jennis assured Dylon, that if Gazsi was now feeling strong enough to be joining intimately with him, it was a good sign. Full well knowing though, how he and Gazsi often over exerted in the throes of lust, he only had one request. He asked Dylon to be careful and not be aggressive in his need. He must allow Gazsi to set the pace, as he gained in strength and endurance.

Several lights later, Bahari sounded in private to Jennis, that Gazsi looked much brighter and stronger, these recent lights. Jennis did not reply. He just smiled broadly. Seeing this expression, Bahari knew the reason. He embraced Jennis, roaring with pleasure. They went off to their special place, to intimately celebrate the joyous recovery of both their male offspring.

11

As lights came and passed, in the Delmar's tropical place, Gazsi slowly gained in strength and structure. Both Bahari and Jennis were pleased with his recovery. No one though, was happier than Dylon. He finally had his life partner back, in the way that pleased them both.

Gazsi was once again highly driven. As was the norm, for most of their growing cycles, he needed to completely possess Dylon, every dark. Dylon, not quite yet being of age to have mating instincts, loved the intimacy of once again feeling enveloped, by Gazsi's strong muscular arms.

By the next full cycle both Bahari and Jennis knew what to expect. Dylon would gain the drive to breed. When this natural development happened, Dylon would out-grow his mostly passive role. Gazsi would have to accept that at times he would also have to submit to Dylon's need to possess, in order to grow their relationship into its adult phase.

During this warm water cycle as in every warm cycle, many of the Delmar females gave forth new life. It was a hectic time. The elder females and healers were kept busy during lights and darks administering to the life givers as they spawned.

The new spawn flourished and grew in the tropical warmth of their birthing place. It was crucial that they gained as much strength and growth as possible during their first cycle.

Later that cycle, the waters started to overheat. While the Delmar thrived in warmer waters, they suffered once the waters became too warm. It became difficult for them to filter their nourishment needs as the hotter waters bred blooms of toxins that were not good for the Delmar's health.

It was now time to gather together and move the entire pod back to their cooler place, to enjoy the cooler more moderate waters. There was a special excitement connected to this migration. Once they returned to their cooler place, the light would be fast approaching when they would take part in the much anticipated mating festival.

Just when The Delmar pod was expecting the Elders to signal to begin preparation for the upcoming migration, a tragedy occurred. The Elders drew Jennis and Bahari aside to communicate. Four of the almost-breeding-aged males had become severely ill. On investigation, it was learned that this group of young males had been spending their free lights exploring a previously not used lagoon. It had been traditionally avoided as it bordered a nearby dry place that was heavily populated with the pillared ones.

The Elders requested that Bahari and Jennis investigate. Gazsi and Dylon were now mature enough and capable of attending to the safety and needs of the little ones, for at least part of a light.

Just as the following light dawned, Jennis and Bahari entered the lagoon. It was immediately apparent that it was a dangerous place for the Delmar. Taking care not to be seen, they drifted to the surface. It was all too obvious. Where the surf touched upon the dry place, pillared creatures were in the process of constructing a massive structure. It had two stone like towers, both of which were billowing smoke.

They belched like the underwater fire pillars of the tropical places. Below the surf line, Bahari and Jennis observed large cylinders entering the water. On closer inspection, the cylinders were bursting forth with a clouded effluent. It had a strange bitter taste, causing their lips to burn. Jennis and Bahari immediately backed off and surged towards the open water.

As they retreated it was obvious, the cloud substance was ever so slowly filling the lagoon. Looking once more above the waves, they could see that the pillared creatures were in the process of adding two more large cylinders, into the surf. This could only mean more poison entering their world.

Returning immediately to the Elders, Jennis and Bahari made known what they had seen. Early the following light, they guided a delegation of Elders towards the lagoon. Cautiously approaching it, they became aware that the cloud had now all but filled the entire lagoon. It was billowing outward with the constant movement of the current. They knew that the cloud of poison would slowly seep into the surrounding sea. It had nowhere else to go.

Already there were many small sea creatures floating around. They were either already lifeless, or in the throes of an agonizing end.

The Elders observed this scene in horror. Then they quickly returned to their lairs to gather the entire body of elders. They had a conference to decide on a plan. Early the following light, a signal was sounded through the entire Delmar community. A council was about to convene. Hearing the low water-borne sounds, all of the Delmar ceased what they were doing and quickly proceeded to their meeting place.

It was a sorrowful day for the Delmar community. They were told that one of the youths had succumbed to his illness. Thankfully, the other youths involved were not as severely ill. It was hoped that by moving them to a safer place, they would recover.

The Elders also announced that although it was not quite time, the entire community was commanded to immediately prepare to leave for their cooler place. They were also warned that in preparation for their journey, they must gather and transport any special possessions that they wished to keep. Every Delmar was saddened to hear that they would not be returning to this, their historic place of warm festivals and birthing lagoons.

But before the migration could happen, the Delmar gathered, to comfort the breeding life givers of the lost youth. Together as a community they conveyed the young Delmar male, now wrapped lovingly in an ornate woven cocoon of sea growth, to a special resting place, deep below the waves.

As was their tradition, it took the combined strength of several younger and stronger males to properly prepare the resting place. The lost Delmar must be ensconced deep beneath a heavy rock bed, to ensure his safe, and, most importantly, hidden resting place.

Bahari and Jennis, like all of their community, had lived their lives in this warm place. They were saddened that by next warm cycle, the elders would have located a new gathering and birthing place that was safe for all. It was now painfully clear that their many-generations-birthing place was now deadly, because of the activities of the pillared creatures.

Many younger Delmar came forth to the Elders, sounding the same question. By their nature, they would never cause a situation that endangered the lives of the dry place creatures. They could not understand how it could be that all life below the waves was continually being threatened in return.

Some even reasoned that if the Pillared ones were aware of the Delmar's existence, they would take more care in protecting them. The Elders could only reply, using the demise of the giant air breathing ocean creatures as examples. They trusted the pillared ones and happily became known. In response they were systematically destroyed, rather than honored and protected.

In the midst of the preparations, Delja and Zeeman approached the Elders council. Delja was in severe distress. She was concerned that by future cycles, her own watery surface meeting place could also be unsafe. She knew that it too was dangerously near a gathering place where the pillared ones lived. She was in severe emotional pain, lest the reunion with her pillared lover and their little male spawn could not happen.

The Elders assured Delja that she need not worry right away. Because of the currents that traversed the vast waters, if the nearby pillared ones created a similar activity near her cooler meeting place the currents there would help. The bulk of any poisoned water would weaken and generally flow away from her favored meeting area.

The elders promised Delja that in future they would be more vigilant in monitoring the activities of the pillared ones in both their areas of resting. They promised her that for the next full cycle at least, she would be reasonably safe, to have her brief reunion. But they were aware that the pillared populated community near where she gave birth was ever growing. They therefore resolved to be more vigilant in order to protect Delja and her spawn.

They did, however, instruct Delja that on that next meeting light, she should attempt to somehow signal to her pillared lover that it might no longer be safe to meet in the usual place. She would have to find a more secluded place further away from the pillared community. The Elders had no idea how Delja could do this, but they impressed that she must try and make him understand. In future cycles Delja and Jasper should meet much further away from their intimate meeting place. She had to also try and make her pillared lover aware of the possible horrors and poisons that the pillared ones were carelessly discarding into the waters.

As they explained all of this to Delja, they were amazed. Rather than looking worried and concerned, she was now smiling broadly. One Elder questioned Delja's reaction to this dangerous situation. It was a major challenge for a Delmar to attempt direct communication with a dry place creature, let alone being clearly understood. The Delmar had no means of understanding and using the pillared ones sounds. Sensing that she knew more than they realized, they pressed Delja for information.

All of the elders present were thrown into complete shock and horror, as Delja revealed her discovery. For the first time in Delmar history, they might have the means to communicate directly with the pillared ones. This startling news caused both amazement and feelings of impending doom among the elders. Many feared that they would be preyed upon and destroyed, like the giant air breathing creatures of the deep.

But at the same time, the concept of direct communication with dry place creatures opened up a long list of possibilities. Not all of these were deemed to be positive. If Delja was correct in her belief, this little spawn of hers had the possibility of altering Delmar history.

The possibilities in this situation were endless. If Ennis actually did retain and develop his communication skills, it would be an amazing feat of evolution. At the same time, all were in agreement. This could either create a new exciting chapter for Delmar society, or be the cause of their total destruction.

66 Nino Balistreri

12

The elders rushed everyone to prepare and move at once. It took more than eight lights to travel the distance. They had to follow, and in places, fight the currents to get to their cooler place. Progress was always slow when the entire community of Delmar moved together. The fully grown and older youth, by tradition, kept pace with and assisted the elders and the very young spawn, all of whom were either too weak or too small to traverse the long distance quickly. Because they were migrating sooner than usual, the warming currents were not yet running strong enough to assist them in their journey.

This was an especially difficult migration, being an unusual and stressful time. As a community, they also had to manually propel the three severely-ill youth. All of them were extremely weak, still suffering the effects of the pillared creature's waterborne poison. Each adult Delmar, male and female, as well as assisting others for the first time, also had to bear the burden of transporting treasured belongings. These would need to be transported again at the end of the cool cycle to their new, yet-to-be-chosen warm, berthing, home.

The stress was evident on all, as they slowly moved. As in every migration, Elder males went forth ahead to ensure that no dangers or pillar-created obstructions lay in their path. There was the ever-present danger of the enveloping of the gathering webs that the pillared creatures used to scoop entire communities of unfortunate sea creatures from the depths.

They also had to guard against attacks of predators from the deep. In many areas the Elders sent forth deep waterborne sounds warning the Delmar community to alter their course. This need to maintain safety for all Delmar added a great many lights to their stressful journey.

When they finally reached the safety of their cooler place, it took many lights, before everyone was at ease. They had migrated much earlier than usual. The currents had not yet shifted. Their cooler place was still more frigid than they were comfortably used to. It was stressful for the community of female Delmar. They bore the added task of keeping the newly spawned warmly and safely enfolded among their intimate groupings.

Because they had traversed north earlier than usual, it had been necessary to make use of their deeper, warmer and more-sheltered places. There were vents opening from the sea floor that gave forth continual flows of warm water. These places were darker than they preferred but safer, at least until the time of raging cold waters and horrible swirling winds ended. It took over forty lights, before the water currents and temperature altered enough. Once this happened, they were able to rise to their traditional places and finally settle in.

Thankfully, during this time, there were only three such torrents, none of which were overly severe. During these cooler darks, it was the responsibility of every Delmar breeding male and life-giver and their partners to protect their intimate pod. They had to set their personal needs aside and concentrate on keeping the little ones warm and safe. When the waters finally heated slightly, the older spawn could be relied upon to enfold the little ones in the comfort and safety of their sleep gathering, during the darks.

Until this time came, it was Jennis and Bahari's responsibility to organize the older youth. They positioned them all, creating a snug enveloping of themselves and their elder spawn. In the center of this intimate living enclosure, the little ones happily slept each dark through, in total comfort and warmth.

The entire Delmar community rejoiced, when the elders decreed that it was now warm and safe enough. The waters had warmed and the raging storms had passed. They could finally spread out and surge upward to their favorite lagoons. In celebration of this, a special festival was held, to mark their safe arrival.

To add to the festivities, the Elders, as a governing group, were proud to present the three youths who had been ill. They looked weak and thin, but oh so happy to be alive. Obviously, all three were now well on their way to full recovery.

Lights proceeded as they had traditionally done in the cooler waters. It was a whole new world for the little ones. Most had either not been spawned, or had been still tightly enfolded in their birth giver's warming arms when they had left for their warm lagoons. These were the spawn that had arrived early, before the mass migration to their tropical birthing place.

The Delmar mating festival took place during the cooler water part of their cycle. This by natural design caused the creation of a new generations of spawn. They as a rule appeared during the tropical water half of their cycle. It was better that way, for the giving of a new life. When it came time for birthing, a place that afforded comforting warmer waters made it easier and safer to keep the newborn spawn both healthy and happy.

The Elders and spawning couples were kept busy gathering, feeding and educating the little ones in this less brilliant world. It contained new and different delicacies that the young had never experienced, as well as new dangers in both flora and fauna. For the young ones, these hazards had to be learned about and carefully avoided.

For the entire lights of the warming festival and gathering play times, Bahari and Jennis were pleased to witness Gazsi's activities. He was intensely observing the now-breeding-aged females. They agreed that by the upcoming mating festival, Gazsi would not only be fully healed, but also strong enough to take part in the choosing of a partner as well as the mating rituals.

Exploring their familiar depths, it was evident that the raging water had altered the mostly rock-strewn bottom. There was some damage to two of the shallower reefs. Bahari and Jennis also found three places where the scattered remains of previously unseen ancient pillared ones' crafts were now exposed.

Probing these sites, Bahari and Jennis found signs that one of these craft carried large amounts of shiny metal objects. They gathered a collection of items to give as gifts to the Elders and their own breeding partners.

Signals were passed around. The Elders wished a meeting with the breeding life givers. Once all of the adult Delmar were present, the Elders made their announcement. The Elders had over the cycles been aware of the possibility, of having to move the warm cycle place of their Delmar pod. For many cycles now, the nearby pillared ones had been continually encroaching on their watery resting place. The Elders had, in previous cycles, explored many locations, deep below the distant waves. Some proved to be suitable and others not.

During this current cool cycle, the suitable sites would be revisited by delegations of elders. It was up to the Elders to determine which presented a longer-term possibility for their community to safely exist in. It would need to be a new permanent location for the warm half of their future cycles. It also had to provide the privacy that the birth givers would need to safely bring forth new life.

As lights progressed, the entire Delmar community settled into their routine. To distract from the current events, the Elders planned three extra festival lights. At each of these festivals, Bahari and Jennis had to do double duty, caring for their younger spawn, while at the same time keeping an eye on Gazsi. He was daily growing stronger. On festival or play days, he was now beside himself. He could be seen rushing through the water, exerting himself beyond his limits, to fully partake in the activities.

His furious exertion had a purpose. Gazsi was observing and trying to impress, the coming-of-age females. Some were flattered and excited by Gazsi's muscular prowess. Others were thrilled when they were the object of his attention. Other young female Delmar though were quite totally alarmed by his daring closeness and piercing gazes.

This was a first for both Bahari and Jennis. To be ushering one of their spawn into full maturity was truly a challenge. Both had been assured by the Elders that Gazsi's furious activity was quite normal for this stage in his development. Bahari and Jennis had long ago forgotten about their emotional state when they went through their own coming-of-age, and first mating cycle.

As the mid lights of the cooler cycle approached, the Elders called the breeding males and females together for a conference. They had chosen a new safe, warm home, for their entire pod gathering. The elders explained that in ancient times, it had been a large, pillared creatures gathering place. It had sunk deep below the waves during a horrible shaking of the ocean floor and nearby dry place. Unlike their now unsafe birthing home, this one contained a vast amount of structures. They were told that many structures had fallen and been mostly destroyed, in the terrible upheaval. But many partial structures had survived.

The Delmar community was assured. The new resting place would afford vast amounts of pillared play areas to occupy the youth. It would also give them ample special places, in which to gather and protect their spawn. They also addressed the practical concerns of the breeders and life-givers. Every breeding Delmar was promised that this tropical place, while not as colorful as their traditional lagoons, would be rich in their oral needs. It afforded all Delmar breeders a more than ample supply of readily available nourishment for their young spawn to grow and flourish.

Bahari posed a real concern that if it had been a major settlement, the pillared creatures would be around this sunken place, to explore. He was assured that in Delmar history, no pillared creatures had ever found this place. It lay deep enough, tucked under a massive rock outcropping.

The Elders sounded to Bahari that in order to reach it, a pillared creature would have to travel through a maze of giant rocks. They would find it all but impossible to navigate a way through the tight passages. These eventually opened into the massively large cavern that housed the structures. It was visibly and physically hidden from every angle, including from above.

They were told that the vast gathering of structures had slipped below the waves in two large sections. This made it easy for the Delmar to settle in. One area would be designated by the Elders as being a resting place for the male population. The other would provide protective enclosures, for the females to give birth and raise their young in.

The passage to this new home was longer than their Delmar pod was used to. During the passage time it was necessary to stop three times for several lights in order to provide rest and nourishment for the entire pod. As they journeyed, there were many areas to avoid. Each time the advance Delmar guides sensed a danger, they signaled for the entire pod to go deep and rest while they explored. As always there was the ever present danger of large pillared ones' crafts and their massive gathering webs. The route took them near many dry places. These places tended to be more developed and filled with pillared ones resting places. Bahari, Jennis and many of the breeding Delmar pairs were concerned that moving and settling in this part of the waters might not be a wise decision.

On arrival, they were all surprised at the enormity of their new place of refuge. All were hopeful that this would prove to be both a safe and long term solution to their needs. It took many lights to settle in and create each individual pods own space, to nurture their life partners and spawn.

The sunken pillared ones gathering place was enormous. The Delmar community could only wonder at how many pillared ones had lived there. It was the first time in their existence that they could physically explore the kind of structures that the pillared ones used as their settling places. It was also a first for most Delmar to observe and handle many of the articles that the pillared ones used within their resting places.

As promised, the youth were excited. This new resting place had massive rows of columns and archways to surge through. It would serve them well during their festival lights, as well as special games.

As well as the many structures and pillars in their new birthing place, they had amazing evidence that this had been a pillared ones' important resting place. At first it was shocking for the Delmar to come upon. But they soon became relaxed among the stone images of pillared ones.

One large and impressive form especially entranced the Delmar males. It stood upright under a large arch at the entrance of a many pillared circle. It was a stone image of a long-haired, extremely muscular pillared creature that also had massive facial hair. His form was all but uncovered, draped only in what presented like a thin covering that draped from one shoulder and barely covered his breeding areas. His hair being long looked more like the Delmar males' hair but it did show signs, that in spite of its length, it had been shaped and formed. Also in stone, his head was topped with an ornate head piece that encircled and held his ample hair in place.

Several of the elders and mature Delmar were familiar with these ornate circles. They had seen them before in the wreckage of ancient surface craft that were laden with shiny treasures. It was a revelation for all to realize that these were articles to be worn on a head. They all agreed that these circles must signify extreme importance, as they had never witnessed a pillared one on a floating craft or bathing in the water with these circles on their heads.

The magnificent and proud looking stone image stood upright and held a long weapon. Instead of one sharpened point, it held a formation with three extremely sharp points. The Delmar males who were the protectors in dangerous times found it fascinating. They wondered how they might create such instruments.

Being so deeply shrouded by giant overhanging ledges, the light was not as intense as in their old warm place. This however did not affect the Delmar. Like their sense of hearing, their vision below the waves had the extreme clarity that most creatures of the deep shared.

The sea growth was abundant in these warm waters. Much of it was similar to their previous tropical place. Some of it however was new and strange. The entire Delmar population had to learn what nourishment was safe to consume. It was obvious, by the mature flora and abundance of resident sea creatures, that this place had slipped below the surface many very long cycles ago and had lain undisturbed for the entire time.

13

Not a great distance away, the Delmar males could observe large stretches of sand along the dry place. Each of these dry sand areas was backed by tall, massively large structures. These had to be the settling places for many pillared creatures. The sand along the water's edge was filled, every light, with great numbers of these creatures.

The Delmar observed differences though from other heavily populated sand places. It seemed that at this place, the pillared creatures were segregated in groups. On most of the sand stretches, the creatures wore coverings. The majority of these were extremely brief in nature. On several other sand places, the pillared creatures, male, female and their spawn, lay in the sun, swam and played, completely uncovered. There was one area of sand between the two, where it was mixed. In these places, everyone seemed at ease. Some wore coverings over their breeding areas and others not. All of these new sights had to be observed carefully. With the large number of upright creatures both in and out of the water, the danger was high; a Delmar might be spotted.

In one of the areas, further along the dry place, the currents, combined with the sloping of the water's bed, created a continual surge of giant surf crashing against the dry place. Most of the Delmar youth had only been aware of raging surf when the dark torrents engulfed the waters. This was the first time that they were experiencing it rising from mostly calm waters to great heights as it roared towards the dry place. What made it so strange to the Delmar youth is that the raging towers of water were happening on a sunny, warm light.

Rather than avoiding the raging danger as the Delmar would do, pillared males and females could be observed a long way out, floating on the water's surface. On close inspection, they were not however floating on their own or supported by the usual variety of pillared ones crafts. But instead, each pillared creature was laying afloat on a long, narrow floating object.

When the water rose to an enormous height, they could be observed upright on these objects. The creatures were using their pillars and weight to maneuver themselves, while suspended on the upper ridge and inner face of the massively churning water.

It was, at first, shocking for the Delmar to see them tumble and crash below the surf, then surface and remount their floating objects. As always, the Elders knew what was happening and how it should be handled. Many of them had observed this activity when they had explored this location as a possible new warm birthing place.

For continued safety, the elders set watches to keep eyes on the situation. One watch was positioned among the nearby rock outcroppings, to be an early warning, in case deep swimming pillared creatures attempted to approach their new settling place. For safety, each pod was instructed to search out a fast route to exit their new resting places. This also was important should there ever be another shaking of the ocean floor, or an attack by the predators of the deep.

A second watch was set, to observe the pillared creatures on their floating structures, especially during the lights that produced larger than usual rolling towers of water. With one elder supervising the watch on these lights, it did not take long for the predicted to happen. Early one light an exceptionally large wall of water rose from the depths. Many pillared creatures were on their structures balancing, ready to travel the depths of its massive inner surface. One youthful creature with long flowing fair hair, suddenly tumbled over and over in the enfolding of the wave.

Each Delmar rescuer in turn cringed, as the pillared male youth brutally collided several times with his floating structure. The sensitive hearing of the Delmar enabled them to hear the pounding impacts on his body. Gazing deep inside the wave, they saw one of his pillars rip free from the line that held him secured to his craft. Instead of struggling furiously upward, in an effort to reach the surface, as they usually did. This well formed and muscular creature limply sank deeper, almost to the floor of their watery place.

The Elder in charge instructed two Delmar males to approach the surface, to grab the trailing line and hold it tight. They were instructed to keep as deep as possible below, so as not to be detected. Two other Delmar surged deep, quickly catching up with the now fast-sinking male. As they approached, he appeared to be dead. His mouth was wide open and his eyes stared blankly into the abyss. Enfolding him tightly in their arms, flesh against flesh, the Delmar males' senses could feel his life force. It was just weakly beating inside. He had survived up to now. But they knew that his end was near. He would soon perish, unless he reached the air above. One of the Delmar brushed his flowing hair back to observe. There were no vents on the side of his head to help him survive below the surface.

The Delmar males each grabbed an upper arm and a firm grasp of the thin loose covering that shrouded his middle section, protecting his breeding areas. They quickly propelled him towards the surface, hoping that the motion would cause him to come to life. They feared the worst for this creature. Even with their fast surging movement, this male was still completely limp and non-responsive.

In a desperate move to save him, they thrust his muscular form out of the water, slamming him down hard, on his belly, against his floating structure. This action resulted in the needed effect. It caused him to gag and cough, expelling enough of the water that he had consumed. The liquid that was lodged in his breathing passages was obviously preventing him from drawing in much-needed air. In the process of doing this life saving maneuver, the young creature's frail covering had disintegrated, ripping free from his being.

Watching him coughing up water and floundering across his board, as he became aware again, the Delmar males roared with glee. They were observing his bottom bounce around, as his now exposed mating organ flopped back and forth in the surging current. Rather than leave the pieces of his thin bright colored covering behind, floating in the surf, the young Delmar rescuers decided to keep it, as a souvenir of their adventure.

They sent forth vibrations of happiness, as they returned to the deep. Both were wondering how long it would take the young male to realize that he was totally exposed. Like it or not, he was now uncovered, like many who were on the sand and in the water. His Delmar rescuers both agreed, becoming exposed for all to see was a small price to pay for having his life saved.

From time to time as the lights rolled onward, there was a rescue to perform. None had been as dramatic as the first one. Mostly it was a matter of gathering the severed line from a floating structure and making it look as if the surf and currents caused it to angle back towards its lost owner.

Early one light, the Elder in charge of the surf rescues gathered the six Delmar males who were in his charge. Several deep predators were paying more than usual attention to the pillared creatures. He instructed the Delmar to dive deep and retrieve the instruments that they used to protect their lairs.

Their plan was simple. Each time a deep predator made its move, rushing at a pillared creature with the intent to attack, they began the first of two actions. As the predator neared the surface and its intended victim, two or more Delmar males quickly surged towards the dangerous creature from below. They quickly thrust it upward, so that its forward motion caused it to breach the water's surface. This action made it visible to all of the pillared creatures, both on their floating structures and on the dry sand place.

It worked several times, frustrating attacks. But just as the many pillared creatures were frantically trying to reach the dry place for safety, it happened. A larger-than-most creature of the deep surged forward. It was fast approaching a pillared male. The male was aware and obviously in distress. He was observed, desperately thrashing his structure towards safety.

Just before the predator reached for the young male with its ragged jaws open wide, four Delmar in a group rushed at it from below. This creature was too large and heavy for the Delmar males to propel above the water's surface. They had no other option left but to attack.

In unison, the Delmar protectors forcibly thrust their sharpened weapons into the soft white underside of the beast. Having penetrated deep into the creature's innards, the Delmar males quickly withdrew their weapons. Now in shock, the creature broke its forward motion and began thrashing. Blood and life were fast ebbing from its body.

The Delmar males immediately dove deep. Most of them knew from experience what would happen next. Distance was crucial; it meant safety for all. The rest of the nearby deep predators tasted blood and, sensing distress in the water, quickly attacked.

It was a horrible scene for the gentle Delmar males to witness, thankfully from a safe distance. The deep predators now turned on their own. In the frenzy of the blood-clouded water, they indiscriminately ripped flesh from the doomed creature. In their madness, they attacked each other as well, creating a mass orgy of blood and death.

The entire area became an uncontrollable feeding frenzy. For two of the younger Delmar males in the rescue group, it was a shocking scene. They had never experienced such physical horror. The younger Delmar males had to be physically held and comforted until they were finally able to settle and let the water flow through their vents normally. The Older males and Elders, while revolted by the scene, had experienced it in the past. They were not as horrified as the inexperienced youth.

It was beyond all Delmar understanding to accept this reality. They lived in a community that revolved around love, trust and peace. The concept of turning on your own with intent to not only destroy but also feed upon was totally outside of their comprehension.

The end result was at least achieved. All of the pillared creatures, being forewarned by the Delmar, had ample time to reach the dry place and safety. Quickly, the sound of surface craft echoed through the deep. Sharp piercing noises could be heard from above. The protectors of the land creatures were dispatching the remaining rogue predators.

14

The entire Delmar community quickly settled into their new surroundings. Everyone seemed happy enough. But none could forget their now abandoned long-time berthing place and the lost male spawn they had sadly left behind.

Lights passed all too quickly in the warm place. The little youth grew larger and stronger in the loving care of their birth givers. The older youth also grew in stature and knowledge as they were guided and taught the ways of the Delmar.

The dry places along the water's edge continued to be filled every light with pillared ones. It was beyond the Delmar's ability to know if they were always the same dry place creatures who lived in the tall resting places, or if it were a continual procession of different creatures.

Surprisingly, the large craft that towed the gathering fibers stayed well away from this area. The elders saw very few large pods of sea creatures moving near this place. It made sense because of all the pillared activity in the water sea creatures would naturally avoid the area.

The elders soon began making plans for the next cycle. Along with the migration to the cooler place and the upcoming mating festival, the time was fast approaching for the changes in their intimate male pod makeup. Like many other breeding Delmar males, Bahari, like many males in his pod, would soon assume the care and education, of his nearly two-cycle-old male. It meant a total change in their routine. The new spawn would need constant care and protection for at least two more cycles. Then he would be grown and strong enough to join the older spawn in their daily education and activities. He was presented to the Elders two cycles ago, as a newborn spawn. Bahari and Yahaira had chosen the sound Varun to be his.

As was custom, Bahari now spend part of each light with Varun and Yahaira. It was important for Varun to be comfortable in Bahari's arms. He would obviously miss his birth giver's closeness. Over the past many lights, he had been fed less and less of Yahara's life giving fluids. He was now, unknown to him, extracting almost all of his nourishment from the water flowing through his vents.

Added to this, Yahaira kept an ongoing selection of tasty feeding items, gathered from the surrounding reefs. This replaced his continued want and need for the oral satisfaction that was solely provided by Yahara's rich nourishing fluids. It was now up to Bahari to win over his love and trust in the strong arms of his tender care.

The lights finally came when the waters began to overheat. The elders prepared the Delmar for their journey to their cooler place. Bahari and Jennis had much to cope with. Varun was now spending most of every light with Bahari. He would be in Bahari's care for the entire migration. From previous experience, Bahari knew that to travel the great distance, with a little one in his arms, would take several more lights than usual.

Jennis, on the other hand, had Gazsi to deal with. It was all but impossible to keep him focused on helping the younger spawn with their needs. His entire mind and being was racing full out, with thought of the upcoming mating rituals. Meanwhile Jennis was cradling his very tiny Shui in his arms.

Once the Delmar community completed their pilgrimage to the cooler waters, it was time to settle in. The passage had happened with only three changes in their usual pattern and thankfully no dangerous situations. Working as a united pod, Bahari helped care for Jennis's younger spawn, while he introduced Gazsi to the lagoon where the mating festival would take place.

88   Nino Balistreri

15

On the first light of the festival, Gazsi was in a frenzied whirlwind. Bahari and Jennis hoped that it would not take long before he found his true mate. Obviously, in his hyper state, Gazsi had already made himself shockingly well known to the breeding-aged females. Unknown to Jennis, he had already made his most important connection. By mid light, on the first gathering of the festival, Gazsi was observed locked in the arms of Tamaki.

Like Gazsi she was robust and stronger than most. Her hair flowed down her back like a torrent of fiery flame. Jennis was unsure about this match. Gazsi was so intensely strong, both in body and spirit. He knew that Tamaki was of a similar disposition.

Jennis addressed the issue with members of the Elders council, who were the festival masters. They assured Jennis that Tamaki was of no blood connection to Gazsi. They would be a safe, albeit high spirited, physical match. They were all in agreement;

Jennis could expect the future birth of strong healthy spawn, to grow his pod. They did however concur with Jennis. This pairing would definitely be a constant match of strength, endurance and willpower.

By the third day of the festival, the new mating pairs who still hesitated or lingered were given a signal from the elders. It was now time to disappear, to seek their intimate places. Before Jennis and Bahari could wish Gazsi well, he was gone in a flash, with Tamaki surging by his side. In just a few lights, Gazsi and Tamaki re-appeared. They had obviously enjoyed their first lights and darks together in the mating lagoons. As was tradition, they had also chosen a special place where they would always be alone together.

Bahari and Jennis soon realized who was missing. Since the festival had commenced, neither had seen Keone and Nadish. The young males had constantly been inseparable through the cycles. But now they were both of the cycle that should have seen them venturing separately, to choose breeding mates. Bahari and Jennis as traditional Delmar accepted what was meant to be. They would probably never see this loving pair branch out and choose opposites to mate with. Both were happy though, knowing that Keone and Nadish would not exist alone. They had each other to care for and love.

The new mating pair Gazsi and Tamaki performed their duties as they were taught. They spent one light communicating their happiness with Bahari, Yahara, Jennis and Negeen. This was also the light as tradition dictated that Tamaki formally presented Gazsi to her breeding life givers and their life partners. Having completed this most important duty, Gazsi and Tamaki promptly disappeared, back to their secret place. Bahari knew that in just a few lights, they would separate and rejoin their communities.

As this part of the cycle came to a close, Bahari now had Varun fully in his care. He had also happily spent three lights and two darks in Yahara's arms, cavorting in their own secret place. Both Bahari and Yahara had driven themselves to exhaustion, in their lustful pursuit of pleasure. Enhancing their pleasure was the added anticipation of creating a new Delmar life.

The cooler cycle all too soon came to an end. During the last lights of this cooler time the waters often became angry. The raging waters that came several times were not of a horrible nature. This was a rare cycle when the Delmar were not required to take part in a rescue of the pillared ones. The less violent waters had not driven any nearby pillared ones' surface craft into mortal danger.

As the unsettled waters once more began to get frigid, it was time for the Delmar to migrate to their warmer home. By tradition, the Delmar made this journey as a community. The well and fit were charged as always with the task of helping the very old and young. They must keep pace with the pod to ensure their safe arrival. During the onset of the migration, Jennis realized that Gazsi was not hovering nearby Dylon and his siblings, as he traditionally did. In concern for his eldest, he left Bahari with their spawn and sought him out.

It did not take long to find Gazsi. He was moving along, arm in arm with Tamaki. It at first appeared as if she was ill and Gazsi was assisting her. Concerned over Tamaki's health, Jennis carefully moved a bit closer through the pod. He wanted to get a better look, without invading their intimate space.

Observing Gazsi and Tamaki for only a short while answered his question. Gazsi had instantly matured. He was bearing Tamaki's arm, enfolded in his own strong muscular appendage, with an obvious look of concern on his face. Tamaki was not using the fullness of her considerable strength, to propel herself. Gazsi was flexing his strength and muscular mass, to provide enough forward thrust for both himself and Tamaki.

The reason for Gazsi's over compensation, all but erasing her exertion for the migration, was evident. On closer inspection, Tamaki no longer had a hard flat belly. She was showing definite signs that a new spawn was on the way.

Returning to Bahari, Jennis embraced him tightly and happily related the news. Hearing this, Bahari slowly surged over to a lonely looking Dylon, to assure him that he had not been abandoned.

Quick movements were not possible these days for Bahari. He had to cradle Varun in his arms for all of the light and dark, until the journey was completed. Every little while, Bahari allowed Varun to try to surge forward on his own, while holding his hand for support. He was little by little gaining the knowledge of how to maneuver his fin appendages, to cause forward thrust. Bahari could not let go of Varun's hand, at least not yet. While he was now grasping the concept of constant propulsion, he had yet to master the concept of consistent and direct forward motion. Left on his own, Varun jigged and jagged, trying unsuccessfully to achieve a single direction with coordination.

Bahari knew that, in no time, Varun would be able to move and maneuver on his own, but for at least one full cycle, never out of sight of either Bahari or Jennis. By next full cycle Bahari would be able to let his little one spend play times on his own, accompanied by their younger spawn. Varun would, by next cycle, also be able to sleep his darks, enfolded in the warm and comforting mass of their collective spawn.

Bahari, like all Delmar breeding and life givers, were grateful that Delmar spawn came forth with clear vision and the ability to freely pass water through their vents. The ability to absorb the life-sustaining gasses from the water was a natural gift from the moment they came forth.

All Delmar were familiar with the smaller air breathing members of their underwater gatherings. Their spawn came forth like the Delmar spawn. All needed to learn the ability of controlled and constant forward motion. But unlike the Delmar, they required a constant supply of air from above the water's surface. These creatures came forth without vents to filter the needed nourishment and gasses. One important thing that did please the Delmar was that these creatures were also kind and loving. Their spawn loved the excitement of surging through the pillars and arches alongside the Delmar youth.

94   Nino Balistreri

16

This entire cycle would be an intense one for Bahari and Jennis. While Bahari had been going through the process of accepting complete care for Varun, Jennis was also going through the identical process, accepting full care for his two-cycle spawn Shui. This was the first cycle that Bahari and Jennis had to care for two little ones at the same time. Up to this cycle, every time there had been two spawn reaching the two-cycle age, one or the other of their offspring had been female. This made it easier in that they could share the care giving of just one tiny male spawn.

Shui was a concern for Jennis and Bahari. Unlike the other Spawn that Jennis and Negeen had produced, Shui was quite small and frail. He had come forth into their watery world almost forty lights before he should have.

For the first twenty lights, it was feared that Shui would not be strong enough to survive. With Negeen's constant love and caring he did. It was an exhaustive process for her to cope with. Shui was not like other spawn. He could not take his full fill of her nourishment, then rest for a while. He could only take tiny amounts of Negeen's life giving fluids. It meant almost constant feedings, many times during every light and dark. This exhausting task lasted for Shui's first forty lights. Finally, to everyone's joy, the frail spawn began to take a full feedings and then soon slept naturally after.

That first full feeding became a turning point for Shui. From that light on, he gained in strength and size. By the end of his first cycle, Shui was a robust and healthy spawn, although he showed signs of being much smaller in stature than the rest of the newborn Delmar spawn.

Now in the care of Jennis, Shui was continuing to thrive. Jennis did however have to be aware that he needed more intense observation and care than other new spawn. He was also relentless in demanding a constant tactile attachment to Jennis. He hoped that Shui would soon become interested in the older spawn and their activities. He tried many times to encourage Shui to let the older spawn hold him and play with him. Shui adamantly refused to let go of Jennis for even a brief time.

It certainly made the daily accomplishment of his tasks more difficult, having Shui refusing to be released from his arms. In spite of this challenge, Jennis gladly accepted the responsibility of loving and nurturing his tiny spawn.

After observing this behavior for many lights, Bahari, the ever-sensible problem solver, came up with a solution. He floated up to Jennis and Shui, embracing both in his arms. Jennis was unsure as to what he was doing but sensed by the expression on his face and the hint of sounds, that Bahari was trying to help out.

Grasping both Jennis and Shui firmly, Bahari started to slowly spin the three of them around while making happy sounds. Shui thought that this was great fun. Thankfully, he did not get upset when Bahari started to shift the tiny spawn back and forth across Jennis's chest. As the rotations increased, so did the back and forth movement.

After a while, Bahari was shifting Shui all over Jennis's front while slowly widening the arch to slide over his shoulders and around his side. Jennis at this point realized what Bahari was doing. He gladly cooperated by adding to the happy sounds and swirling movements.

Once embracing Jennis from his back, with Shui still wedged between them, Bahari added a new motion. He slid himself and Shui upwards and downwards as if to peek over one, then another, of Jennis's shoulders. Jennis rotated his head back and forth in order to greet Shui with an exaggerated and animated smile as he appeared on each side of his face.

While Shui was still making sounds of glee, enjoying the new game, Bahari added a new feature. He took Shui's arms and wrapped them around Jennis's neck. Prodding Jennis in the back, he urged him to start moving around, while accomplishing tasks with his now freed hands.

Jennis moved forward, even though it was difficult with both Bahari and Shui firmly clinging to his back. Bahari kept urging Shui to look over one then another of Jennis's shoulders, to observe what he was doing. After a while Bahari started to relax his grip.

Meanwhile, Jennis went about the task of gathering tasty bits of sea growth, then feeding it to Shui over his shoulders.

Shui was so fascinated by this new game, he did not notice as Bahari slowly relaxed his grip on them both. In a while, the game was over. Bahari was floating freely, helping Jennis gather, as both fed Shui over Jennis's alternate shoulders.

Shui now had a new fascinating place to cling, where he could safely watch all that was going on around him. Jennis was pleased to be released from constantly holding the tiny spawn in his arms. He now had no care as to how many lights it would take, before Shui grew in confidence. When that happened, he would start to want to interact with and be cared for at times by the other young spawn in their intimate pod.

17

As the lights progressed through the cycle, changes occurred. Shui was happy and thriving, but still clinging to Jennis. Bahari decided that it was now time for Shui to widen his environment. Varun had for a long while now enjoyed being cared for and playing little ones' games with the other young spawn.

Bahari decided that it was now time for Shui to take part in the other young spawns' activities. He had Jennis remain still while he hovered behind him, just an arm's length away. He turned his back and dangled one of Shui's favorite tasty treats over his shoulder so that Shui could see. It encouraged him to reach for it. Shui tried several times but in the end could only reach the treat if he let go of Jennis's neck and transferred to Bahari's neck. Then Jennis did the same.

As soon as it was evident that Shui saw this as a game, they ever so slowly started to widen the gap between their backs.

Gurgling with glee at this new activity, in no time they had Shui thrusting under his own power a fair distance to reach his goal. From that light on, Shui was never afraid to let go of Jennis or Bahari when his attention was drawn to an interesting object or activities of the other spawn.

It was not too many lights along when Bahari noticed a change in Dylon's attitude. As if over one light and dark he became pensive and quiet. Bahari questioned Kye, the healing Elder. He was concerned that Dylon was not well.

The Elder assured him that all was well. Bahari had only to wait till the upcoming play light festival and all would be revealed. As always, the ever wise Kye knew.

On that festival light, Dylon could be observed almost in a trance state, observing the females of his cycle. Having recently gone through the process with Jennis's Gazsi, Bahari happily knew what to expect. The balance of this cycle and the next would build Dylon's confidence and prepare him for his coming of age.

It was good that Dylon now had a new interest to fuel his drive. It so obsessed him that he barely noticed the change in Gazsi's routine. Gazsi was not only dividing his attention between his duties in the pod and Dylon. Now, on every possible occasion, he was being with Tamaki and their tiny female spawn. The coming forth of his little spawn had been a traumatic experience for Gazsi. Seeing Tamaki in the painful throws of giving life, Gazsi was in shock. He needed almost as much comforting and care from the elder healers as Tamaki required. The elders assured a distressed Gazsi that all was well and that he would get used to this traumatic event.

As was custom with the Delmar, the birthing life-givers chose the new spawn's sound. That light Gazsi fell even deeper in love with Tamaki. She honored him, by giving their new female spawn the sound Marella in honor of Gazsi's lost birth giver.

This choice also pleased Jennis. The new tiny Marella would soften the saddened spot in his heart, where he harbored the memory of his lost first love. Marella was a strong healthy spawn who came forth with a thick head of hair in the same flaming hue of Tamaki's long flowing tresses. This pleased both Gazsi and Tamaki.

As soon as Marella became aware enough to be released from Tamaki's arms, Gazsi went most lights to spend a short while with her. He slowly taught Marella how to propel and maneuver her little structure. It would still be a long while, almost two cycles, before she would be strong and confident enough to propel through daily activities totally on her own. But Gazsi was so enjoying teaching her that Tamaki didn't object. Actually she enjoyed the freedom that having a rest from constant care gave her.

Almost half way through the cycle, sad news circulated in the Delmar community. Kye, the head of the Elders, was ill. He had served for many cycles as leader of the gathering of Elders. His demise had been more or less expected, as he had achieved a number of cycles that was much greater than the norm for a Delmar male. But still, it was a sad time for the entire pod.

For all of Bahari and Jennis's cycles, Kye had been the respected healer and leader of the entire Delmar pod. Gazsi especially felt a close bond with Kye, as he believed he owed his very existence to Kye's expert care following his horrible experience of crashing against the dry place.

Kye had governed with no more than the love, wisdom and understanding that all Delmar naturally expected. He had outlived both his breeding and life partners. The entire pod rotated and kept a loving vigil during light and dark through the time that Kye's life force slowly faded away. It was a truly sad day for the entire pod of Delmar as they conveyed Kye to his resting place. With the entire pod in procession, Kye was carried forth to his final rest by many generations of his own female and male spawn.

After the traditional number of lights, it was now time to elect a replacement to lead the Elders. The community of Elders was comprised of older mature male and female Delmar. After much deliberation, the Elders made their decision. For the first time in any known history, a female Delmar was chosen from among the community of Elders. Her sound was Taras.

A special festival light was planned for Taras to be presented formally to the entire Delmar pod. At the end of the ceremony, Taras made an announcement. Her first task as Supreme Elder will be to confer and choose a new Elder to replace her in the council of rulers. It must be a Delmar whom everyone deemed worthy enough to be brought into their governing fold.

Twenty lights later the Elders announced a festival light. Once the entire Delmar pod was in attendance, Taras and the Elders went before the gathering. Taras proudly announced that they had chosen a new Elder. The anticipation was exciting for every Delmar. Traditionally, the choosing of a new Elder was a closed decision made by the Elders with just a message to all, once a choice had been made. This would be the first happening that a festival for all Delmar was part of the process.

When Taras floated forward into the Delmar gathering and grasped Jennis's hand, the surprise was complete. She led him back towards the gathering of Elders. Jennis and Bahari were overjoyed with the decision. It would mean a great deal more responsibility for Bahari. He would have to care for and teach their collective spawn, while Jennis was required to be with the Elders, but he gladly accepted the challenge.

The entire pod sounded their pleasure and acceptance of the Elders' choice. Jennis was young, strong and wise. Every Delmar in the pod agreed; Jennis would be an excellent Elder, who would be able to serve the pod well for many long cycles.

18

For the next many lights, Jennis spent a lot of time with each of the elders. As much as he already knew about the governing of the pod, he still had a lot to learn about their decision-making process. He, like many Delmar, assumed that the supreme elder made most of the decisions that he announced. In fact, the supreme elder only announced the collective decisions of the entire group of elders.

Thirty lights after Jennis joined the elders council, the pod had visitors. A delegation from another pod approached. Their pod had always been aware that the vast waters contained a large number of pods like theirs. Jennis knew that because this other pod occupied not-too-distant areas of the vast waters; they had come in contact with these other Delmar several times in his many cycles. The delegation requested to meet with the pod's Elders.

Settling with them, Taras and her council heard their story of tragedy. Near their warmer home lived a large community of deep predators. In many generations there had seldom ever been problems.

Unfortunately, in recent cycles their nearby pillared creatures had acquired larger craft with immense gathering fibers. Over several cycles they had decimated the local population of sea life. The consequence of this was that the deep predators were starving. In desperation they took to attacking the pillared ones when they found them in the water and were also targeting the Delmar gatherings. The predators were too many and too strong for the Delmar to repel.

The final attack five lights before had been the most devastating. In the battle to defend their pod many Delmar were destroyed, including their Leader and over half of their Elders council.

It was decided that the safest way to survive was to leave their long time home behind and seek the security of another pod. They hoped to find a pod that was organized enough and had a resting place that was large enough to absorb the additional Delmar.

The Elders heard their tale of woe. They certainly knew the feeling of having to flee their long time home because of the actions of the pillared ones. Taras conferred with her council of Elders and made a decision. Both their warm water home and their cool festival home were vast. Their settlement places had ample nourishment and structural security to protect an enlarged pod.

Jennis also reminded the Elders group that it had been many generations since new blood was mixed into their breeding community. All agreed that an influx of new Delmar breeders and life-givers could only make the pod more diverse and much stronger.

Returning to the delegation, Taras welcomed them to bring their pod in all haste, but to choose a time of the light or dark when the deep predators were not active. It was important that they not be aware of the route taken, lest they follow the pod to their new home. Five lights later the Delmar of the devastated pod began arriving.

Once the new pod were all secured in their midst, Taras divided up her elders and older Delmar males and females. The strongest were charged with guarding the entrances approaching their gathering place. She was in fear of the predators finding their way. Because of the hidden openings to their grotto, the resting place was safer and easier to protect than their former open lagoon would have been.

The balance of the adult Delmar was set to work assisting the new pod to settle. Each individual grouping needed to create a special place to settle and rest. The youth that had lost their breeding protectors needed to be spread out among the gatherings so that they could be educated and enfolded for safety.

Because so many of the new pod's males and female breeders had been lost in the battle with the predators, there were many youth to care for. Taras and the council carefully chose Delmar male and female couples that had appropriate ages of little spawn to blend with.

In the end there was just one pair of spawn left to place. They were special, a very unusual happening for the Delmar. In no recent history had it been known that a Delmar female had spawned not only two little ones at once, but in this case two identical little ones. They were just approaching two cycles. Their sounds were Kato and Kawai.

The entire Elders council agreed. It was crucial to keep the pair of spawn together. The tiny ones had suffered enough trauma and loss in their short existence. They were so unhappy, constantly looking in every direction for their lost life-givers. They were too young to understand what had happened. No amount of comfort given by the general community of female or male Delmar could ease the pain of their loss nor lift their spirits. During each dark they could be heard by all as they called out in horror wanting the comforting embrace of their birth giver.

Taras and the elders' council debated for several lights over this problem. There were no groupings that could easily absorb two who were so little and so extremely needy. It would take a great deal of intense comforting and concentrated care to overcome their horrible loss. They were so much smaller and frailer than most spawn of their birth cycle. The entire pod was already burdened with as many extra spawns as they could safely cope with.

It was Jennis who came up with the perfect solution. He addressed the council. He made them aware that they had bypassed one Delmar paring that had no spawn of their own and never would. To everyone's surprise he was exactly right. It was perfect. All of the Elders were amazed that in this trying time they had missed taking the pair into consideration. There was certainly no shortage of love and caring between them and more than enough strength to provide and protect.

Early the following light, Jennis sought out the pair and brought them before the elder's council. At first they were afraid that there was trouble, but he assured them that it was good.

Presented in front of the entire council of elders, Keone and Nadish were both stunned and overjoyed, when they were presented with their very own tiny pair of identical Delmar spawn to love, teach and protect. It was a new first for the Delmar society, one that the elders knew would set a precedent for the future.

After twenty lights and darks, with no sightings of predators, Jennis, as head of the guard detail, slowly eased the watchers. In ten more lights with all being safe and well, he reduced the protector's watch to the amount that was normal.

The next task for the Elders council was to take a census. Taras gathered her Elders. They worked out how many elders represented how many Delmar in their own pod. Then they met with the surviving Elders from the new pod. The number of surviving Delmar gatherings were large enough to have twenty Elders. Unfortunately only twelve had survived the predators' attack.

With Jennis' help Taras devised a plan. A special festival would be held for the new group's Elders to choose eight new Elders from within their original pod. Once they were incorporated into the receiving group of Elders, the rules would change. In future it was decreed that they would all be part of a new enlarged pod. There would not be two groups of Delmar, or two groups of Elders. By Taras' decree they would be one large group of both Elders and Delmar.

As the resettling happened and the new enlarged Elders group became comfortable working together, Taras planned to carefully make them aware of the amazing situation with Delja, her pillared lover Jasper and their pillared spawn Ennis. They were still not entirely sure how it would evolve. It was believed that if done carefully, the Delmar would be able to convey danger warnings through Jasper and Ennis. The pillared population must be made aware of the devastation of the waters and its resources. But they must believe that Jasper was simply a self made protector of the waters and its inhabitants.

The pillared ones must be warned but at the same time not informed, of how Jasper came to have his information. The council of Elders still believed, as generations before them did: to be known to the dry place creatures would only bring suffering and death to all Delmar.

All went well for a while. Collectively the Delmar guarded their resting place and watched for pillared ones who needed rescuing. The deep predators had not shown interest in the pillared ones for a long while. The elders believed that it was mostly because their numbers had been horribly devastated by the violent incident that destroyed a great number of them.

Many lights later a group of young Delmar exploring the wider areas a fair distance from their warm home ran into danger. Often groups of responsible youth were given permission by the Elders to explore further depths and if possible bear greetings to other Delmar pods. They were exercising the usual caution, aware that several large surface craft were nearby. They knew the importance of being on guard. Suddenly they were shocked by a horrible sound. Again and again it bellowed through the watery deeps. It was extremely painful for the Delmar to hear.

The shock waves surged though the waters, leaving them confused. The sound was so encompassing, it was difficult to determine what direction it was coming from, or, in fact, if it was coming from several directions at the same time. This prevented them from escaping in an opposite direction. Suddenly there was one excruciating eruption, sending the entire group swirling in circles of pain. They were all surprised when the sounds abruptly stopped, but were grateful that they had all survived.

Using their strong vision, they could just barely see a large object as it slowly settled to the ocean floor. The group of young Delmar adventurers was horrified. As it traveled downward it belched with flames and convulsed with horrible explosions.

None of these young Delmar had been to the watery places where flames and explosions burst from craters in the water's floor. It was a new horror for them to experience. They waited in fear, safely huddled behind a large outcropping. During the dark that followed, the horrible sounds and fires quieted.

As the following light grew stronger, the gathering of Delmar youth slowly ventured forth. Carefully moving towards the object, it soon became obvious. It was a massive surface craft. They were too terrified to go closer. It was still sending streams of air and thick black strands of liquid upwards towards the surface.

Observed from afar it was plainly evident that the giant craft had been violently burst open in several places. There were no reefs nearby that could have caused this damage. The Delmar youth were certainly familiar with death, but they had never in their short existence been faced with the horrors of hatred-fueled death. They concluded that it must be a result of conflict, another emotion that was foreign to them.

There were many pillared creatures strewn around the sea bed in the area of the craft. They were clad in damaged and torn fabric. What remained of it all had a similar hue and color. The Delmar youth had only experienced seeing pillared ones in many colored variations of coverings. They didn't understand why or how all of these lifeless pillared ones could look so identical in their coverings.

The Delmar males, afraid of continued danger from above, left the area immediately. They traveled nonstop for almost two lights and a dark in order to return to the safety of their own pod. Reporting to the Elders, they were commended for their quick action in escaping the area. The Elders knew that the sunken craft was not a pleasure or working craft for the pillared ones. It was a craft designed solely for conflict and death.

They had to educate the youth to accept this reality as their history had dictated. Some of the Elders now believed that the situation might change, now that they could communicate through Ennis. But an equal number of Elders believed that nothing would change. They held to the teachings of Delmar history. They helped the traumatized youth to understand. Like the predators of the deep, it was well believed by the Delmar that pillared ones do not live with love and peace in their hearts. For a strange reason unknown to the Delmar, the dry-place creatures thrive on creating death and destruction above and beneath the waves.

More shockingly for the Delmar, the pillared ones also nurtured hatred and death among themselves in the dry places, as well as upon the great watery surfaces. They continually preyed upon each other to destroy.

The Delmar found it most difficult to accept this. Hatred and willful death were not part of their psyche. The only death they accepted was in protecting themselves and their pillared neighbors from deep predators and wildly raging waters.

19

The joining of the two pods was a difficult process, but as the lights wore on it improved. It certainly took all of the expanded Elders council's efforts to coordinate festivals. It was an amazing situation where so many of the youth were excited by the introduction of unknown breeding possibilities. The expanded numbers also fostered enhanced levels of competition in their games. On festival lights the entire elders group was on high alert to keep everything orderly and, most importantly, safe for all the youth, in spite of their overcharged enthusiasm.

Most importantly, the end of cycle migrations between the warm and cool places took on a heightened level of organization. Because of the enhanced number of Delmar, the first migration took many lights longer than usual. Many of the old and new Delmar pod groupings were burdened by caring for additional spawn that had lost their birth and care givers. Others were assisting members of the new pod who had survived the horrific deep predator attack, but had been left horribly injured or permanently disabled.

Games and competitions held a new level of excitement, as the male and female youth from each pod strove to out-perform the other. Jennis, as festival organizer, as well as the combined Elders group, were looking forward to the next two or three cycles.

By then, there would be enough inter-mating between the two pods to blend together the present generation of older youth. Once that happened, the concept of their pod being made up of two separate entities would fade out as the younger youth matured.

Already, on festival lights, the older youth were getting acquainted with their new opposites. In the past there was always a small group of males hiding in embarrassment with uncontrollable bursting of their breeding organs. Now, on festival days, the surrounding rocks and sea growth were scattered with a great many embarrassed young males.

The youthful males of both pods had been thrust into an over-excited state by suddenly competing before females they did not know and had not grown up with. The females of each pod were also raging in an excited state. Rather than the limited number of males that they had grown up knowing, they now had a larger number of prospective male breeders to choose from.

The first gathering festival for mating was amazing. Taras and the expanded council of Elders could barely keep ahead of all the frantic activity. The deep predators' attack on the other pod had devastated many of the mating caregivers. For the first time in their experience, there were male and female youth with no breeding life givers to guide them through the process of the mating lagoon, or the counseling about what was to come.

Taras and Jennis selected a grouping of younger male and female Elders. They matched them with the older orphaned youth who were about to enter the mating festival. As always in the Delmar pod, no older adult or youth should ever be without the love and care needed to be supported, fulfilled and happy.

The entire council of Elders was whirled into a vortex of activity, just keeping everything sorted and working smoothly. It was most important that no youth be left feeling either unwanted, or unloved. By the fourth light of the mating festival, most of the new mating pairs had dispersed to their special places. Taras, Jennis, Negeen and every other older Delmar finally had a well earned rest.

Added to their stress during this larger than ever festival was Jennis and Negeen's eldest female spawn Almeta. She was now away with her new mate Rodion, exploring the now almost crowded special lagoon. Jennis planned to propose to the Elders council to either seek out a larger lagoon for future mating festivals or designate several lagoons that the youth could choose between, as their own special mating places. With their now enlarged and continually expanding pod, he knew that it would only get harder to carry on in their traditional lagoon.

As the entire pod settled into a routine, plans were made for their first mass migration back to the warm place. The new members of Elders were informed about the routine of guarding their new home as well as monitoring the pillared ones as they rode the towering water on their strange flat board-like crafts. The new Elders were pleased that the deep predator population in this place was not normally aggressive. Only on rare occasions did they take interest, but so far it had only been towards the pillared ones.

Matsya, an original Elder from the new pod, suggested a reason for this. He alone in his pod had witnessed this phenomenon of pillared ones upright on boards riding the high waters. He suggested that as the pillared ones thrashed about a great deal and tumbled out of control through the towering surf, it was confusing to the deep ones. He believed that these primitive creatures did not possess the Delmar level of understanding.

Matsya believed that seeing pillared ones thrashing about appeared to the predators instincts as being creatures in distress. As scavengers of the deep, this action made the pillared ones appear to be fair feeding game. He believed that it fueled the predators confusion because of their severe hunger. Taras and the council of Elders accepted this as a definite possibility. They could not, however, accept the fact that the predators of the deep the same time, turned on to destroy and consume distressed members of their own. That was just too horrific for the Delmar psyche to grasp.

This migration to the warm place took almost two lights longer than usual. The new members of the pod had to be guided. They had to be encompassed and protected among the original pod members. Many of the permanently injured members from the other pod were now healthier and stronger. But because of their injuries, they would always need assistance and special care, especially during dangerous times and migrations.

It warmed every heart in the pod to witness Keone and Nadish as they happily surged along, side by side, their faces beaming with pride, as each held tight to a wide-eyed and, at last, now smiling identical little spawn.

Once at the new warm home, it took several lights to arrange and settle the expanded pod into the hidden grotto of structures. A lot of initial resettling had happened after the new pod had arrived. But because of the large number of new mating pairs who were now expecting the arrival of new spawn, many new resting places were needed.

The original Delmar males were happy. Their numbers were now enhanced by the new members. Watches guarding their settling place and the surf riding pillared ones would be easier to maintain. When raging waters happened, they would be better able to rescue larger numbers of pillared ones in distress.

Jennis and two other Elders helped the strongest of the new males to fashion weapons to fend off deep predators. Searching through the ruins of their new grotto, they were able to find thin flat shafts of shiny metal that had not dissolved. Each shaft, no matter the length, had a pointed tip along with a fine sharpened edge. It took a lot of extra effort to adapt these new strange items, but it was worth it. They now had weapons to guard and protect with, that were sturdier and sharper than anything they had possessed in the past. They gave instructions to the new protectors as to how the operation of diverting the predators was handled, first in distracting and if that failed, finally in attacking to save the lives of their pillared neighbors.

The lights wore on and all remained well with the Delmar pod. The new expanded protectors group worked well together. Each light they returned to the pod with new tales to tell the little ones about the antics of the pillared ones as they rode the raging surf on their little craft. During that warm time the protectors had successfully repelled three attacks of the deep predators as they stalked the pillared ones. It went well all three times. Thrusting the predators above the waves in each case warned the pillared ones' protectors. Their swift action drove the deep predators' off using their explosive weapons.

20

The time of the cooler cycle was soon approaching. Delja and Zeeman were extremely anxious to be reunited with Jasper and Ennis. The Elders decided, Ennis had to be now of an age that he should be able to communicate in both the Delmar and pillared sounds with Delja and Jasper.

The travel through the depths to the new meeting place went without serious mishap. The pod had to make only two changes in course to avoid the massive gathering webs of the pillared ones. They also had an experience that only a few Delmar had ever witnessed. The forward guides had spotted a massive white pillared ones' craft. They had no sooner diverted to be well away from it, when they sensed a large disturbance on the distant surface. At first they were alarmed, but thinking that it could be a large gathering of deep predators. It soon became clear. It was a massive gathering pod of air-breathing creatures that were not much larger than an adult

Delmar. The Delmar were well used to and known by these gentle creatures. They had the same attitude and gentle behavior as the giant air breathing creatures. On occasion, the younger members of these air breathers loved to join in on play times with the Delmar youth. Especially when they were surging around ancient pillars.

As always when they reached the cooler waters, Delja found Jasper waiting on his small craft. He was upright on his pillars, steadying himself against the tall pole that was centered in the craft. This time, as she and Zeeman approached, they were surprised. Ennis was upright beside Jasper, balancing upon his own pillars. Both were uncovered in anticipation of joining Delja and Zeeman in the warm water.

Delja and Zeeman welcomed their pillared family into their arms. Delja wasted no time communicating with Ennis. To her delight, he haltingly translated her sounds into pillared sounds. It took a while for the transfer of the basic idea of the poisoned lagoon and death. It also shocked Jasper to learn that the ever-growing attacks on pillared ones was being fueled by the depletion of the traditional food sources of the deep predators. Jasper agreed that he would become a spokesman for the deep while being careful to not reveal his source of information.

The cycle was also fast approaching, when Gazsi and Tamaki would graduate their tiny spawn Marella. She would be handed over to the community of females to educate. Being so young and only having experienced one mating festival, Gazsi was also anxiously anticipating the upcoming festival of intimacy. On the first day of the festival, Tamaki gave Marella over to a caregiver from her female community and went hand in hand with Gazsi to their secret lagoon. Three lights later an exhausted but happy pair of Delmar returned.

Gazsi took charge of continuing to visit Marella, who was well used to being enfolded in his arms. A saddened Tamaki returned to the activities of her part of the pod. She was feeling the loss of no longer having a little one continually in her care. She still however looked forward to the end of each light when she could cradle and protect Marella through the restful dark.

Her sadness though was tempered by the knowledge that she was carrying a new life within. In just forty lights Tamaki was assured that she was indeed forming a new life for her and Gazsi within her being.

The pilgrimage to the warm place that cycle went without serious difficulty. It did however take several lights longer than anticipated. The reason for this was a continual changing of direction to evade both gatherings of deep predators and the giant fiber menaces that the Pillared ones were dragging deep below their crafts.

Several more adventurist youth had on occasion approached one of these massive gathering structures and discovered a trailing cord. To their shock when one brave youth grasped the cord, it caused the gathering fibers to burst open. Many creatures were released to escape to the deeps, but, sadly, the structure had done its damage. Many more watery creatures had perished in the horrible crushing of the fiber gathering.

The council of Elders on hearing of this daring exploit decreed that in future the youth were not allowed to interfere in this process. They did agree that it was good to save as many watery creatures as possible, but the risk it ran was too great. If a Delmar youth was hurt or became entangled in the fibers, he would be captured and killed by the pillared ones. It would also cause the dry place creatures to have positive proof that the Delmar existed. They had no choice but accept that these large craft existed solely to destroy as many of their water world's creatures as possible.

They did however make one concession to appease the grouping of now saddened Delmar explorers. They gave permission that, in future, if it could be accomplished safely, they could warn away large gatherings of water creatures so as to try and avoid the gathering fibers of the pillared ones.

Soon the time came for Tamaki to give forth her new life. To her and Gazsi's delight the new spawn was male. He had a full head of hair resplendent in the dark color of Gazsi's flowing tresses.

As was custom with the Delmar, the birthing life giver chose the new spawn's sound. It was to be Trai. Within five lights, Delja also gave forth a new male life. As expected, this time he was a full Delmar. There would be no parting or sorrow for her to endure. When it came time to present her new spawn to the community of Elders she conferred with Zeeman. He was in agreement as he now felt the shared love that their three-way union had grown into. With a break from tradition, both Delja and Zeeman bore the new spawn forward to present to the Elders and announce his sound. When requested, they replied in unison, the sound, "Jasper".

After traveling north to the cooler place, the time came to meet with Jasper and Delja's first born Ennis. Delja and Zeeman were afraid of the ever expanding dry place creature's domain. In the short cycle that the Delmar pod spent in the warm place, the pillared ones had begun construction of resting places near the water's edge. They were within a distant view of Delja and Jasper's original meeting place. Observing these resting places, the Delmar were all amazed. The structures were so close and down level to the water's edge. It was agreed by each Delmar that viewed them. Any severe episode of raging waters would without a doubt destroy these structures.

For safety, Zeeman went forth alone to meet Jasper's craft. Delja with little Jasper in her arms, headed further up the shoreline to be well up current from the pillared one's gathering place. Thankfully Jasper understood. Zeeman made Delmar sounds to Ennis and had him translate pillared sounds in response.

Jasper lifted his weight off the sea floor and proceeded to follow Zeeman with his craft. In only a little while they reached Delja who was waiting in a secluded and uninhabited cove. Jasper quickly and gently lowered the weight to keep his craft in place and then again removed his and Ennis's coverings. Sliding over the side, Jasper reached into the craft and lifted a smiling Ennis into the warm water.

Now, everyone was happy, all together in a warm embrace. Delja gave her new spawn's sound to Jasper. He was both surprised and honored to have the tiny Delmar named after him. It was a strange sight for the loving circle to see, as Jasper cradled his tiny Delmar namesake in his watery arms. Delja was thrilled to be able to communicate fully now with Ennis.

For the first time in history, Ennis was able to tell his father in detail about the poisoned lagoon and the death it caused for both the Delmar and sea creatures and how this event was being repeated in all areas of their watery domain. He still did not understand fully what he was relating, but Jasper did. Jasper was horrified that a Delmar youth had been killed along with so much sea life. He promised to speak to authorities and rally his fishing community, to bring the poisoning of waters to everyone's attention. Because his father had been a fisherman, Jasper was well aware of how sensitive ocean life was and how the effluent from industry can easily destroy.

Delja was careful to warn Jasper through Ennis not to reveal how he discovered this information. Jasper readily understood that if he told and was believed, it would only mean danger for the Delmar as well as his own son Ennis who was, in fact half Delmar.

Later that light a happy Delja and Zeeman reported to an amazed gathering of Elders that the message had been delivered. With this historic achievement accomplished, Jennis made a decision. In the next council of Elders, he proposed a shocking plan. As soon as Little Jasper and Ennis are grown enough to freely swim without the constant support of Jasper senior or Delja, they should plan to search out a secluded lagoon for a special meeting time. He believed that Jasper and Ennis should be trusted.

To cement that trust, Jennis proposed that a delegation of young and adult Delmar should hold a small festival on the surface to incorporate the two branches of their existence. It was cautiously agreed, provided a safe, secluded location could be secured. The entirety of Delmar Elders was still terrified that the Delmar should be discovered and destroyed.

21

The much sought after light had come. Dylon had been surging in erratic circles for many lights now, in anticipation of the upcoming festival. He would now be taken to the special place to participate in the meeting and choose his life breeding mate. For all of the recent play festivals he had furiously participated in the activities of the youth. At the same time, he continually surged back and forth, seeking out Gazsi for advice. They could be seen off alone while intensely watching the activities of the other youth, but especially that of the coming of age females.

Bahari and Jennis were pleased that Dylon sought out his life partner for advice in attracting his breeding mate. As breeding life-givers it was best this way. Bahari and Jennis wanted to avoid being embroiled in this most difficult choice. Their only involvement would be by tradition. Once Dylon and a young female made their choice, the Elders must be consulted to ensure that neither is of an identical blood line. The continuing community of Delmar must be kept healthy and strong.

Unlike in Gazsi's case, the first light of the festival did not produce results for Dylon. By the end of the second light it was evident. Dylon was all but fused to the side of a fair haired beauty. Bahari was much relieved to see that Dylon had made his important connection. He certainly hadn't looked forward to another full cycle of Dylon on the loose and yearning. Jennis looked on her with affection; she reminded him of Marella, when he first fell in love with her. He learned that this youthful Delmar females' sound was Gryta.

Bahari, Yahara, Jennis and Negeen all hovered in a happy grouping as they watched Dylon and Gryta surge off towards their own secret lagoon and the beginning of their productive lives. As tradition dictated, three lights later Dylon and Gryta returned to the pod to carry out the meeting and greeting of all the birth givers and life partners who were involved in their existence. Having completed this duty, they quickly surged off, returning to their intimate lagoon. Bahari and Jennis felt assured, there would soon be a new tiny Delmar joining their intimate pod.

The cool cycle progressed without any major events. Both Bahari and Jennis were directed on occasion by the elders to accompany groups of mid-aged youth who asked for permission to explore beyond their pod's usual areas. They happily did so. No pod member wanted to experience another tragedy like the one that took the life of the young male several cycles before.

It was with sad hearts that Delja and Zeeman bid farewell to Jasper and Ennis. The waters had been continually cooling for many lights now. The waters had also grown angrier. Many Delmar birth givers were nearing the light when they would bring forth a new life. It was crucial that it happen in warmer waters for the health and safety of the new spawn.

The migration to their warm resting place passed slowly. Many Delmar birth givers were extremely close to giving forth life. A hurried strenuous passage would endanger the birth givers and their soon to arrive spawn.

The warm cycle that followed produced a large number of new Delmar spawn. This was due to the large numbers of coming-of-age Delmar, as a result of combining the two pods. In honor of this, Taras decided on a new tradition. In the past, birthing couples could approach a group of elders during any function and present the sound for their new little one.

The ending of this warm birthing season would see the first of their new tradition. A special sounding festival took place. Once the entire pod was in attendance, the council of elders formed at the head of the gathering. One by one the birthing life giving pairs came forward and presented their little one. As they handed the newborn over to Taras, they conveyed its sound. Taras then floated above the gathering, holding the little one aloft and announced to all, the sounds of the birth giving Delmar pair along with the sound that the tiny new male or female Delmar would be known as. This brought forth many happy responses from the entire pod.

This cycle the entire pod was relieved. All of the expected spawn had arrived without undue difficulty and were all proclaimed by the healers as being healthy. A birthing cycle, as well as a cool cycle that was filled with happiness and totally devoid of sorrow was a welcomed happening in the Delmar pod.

The activities of the pod were many during this warm time. Caring for the new born and ever growing community of spawn was an ongoing task. The delegated male and female Delmar kept up their non-stop dark and light watches at the entrance to their hidden grotto. During each light, teams of Delmar also monitored the pillared ones as they rode the crests of the towering walls of water.

During this cycle the watchers had to disrupt three attacks of deep predators as they approached the pillared ones. All of the interventions went as planned this cycle. Causing the predators to breach the surface each time gave the pillared ones ample warning to quickly rush to the dry place for safety.

None of the Delmar ever wanted to witness the blood and carnage of the last violent episode. Two of the youngest protectors who witnessed it were so traumatized by the event, they were unable to return to that duty. The elders understood and made sure that these males were assigned to duties that would not be overly stressful.

On each festival and play light, Jennis was happy to observe Keone and Nadish with Kato and Kawai, their little spawn charges. Where, in the past, Keone and Nadish would always stay aside and take little physical involvement in festival activities, they now were right in there taking part in and enjoying every moment of the festivals.

One light a group of youth were having a game of speed as they surged in and out of the pillars in the great meeting space. This sat at the center, half way between the two groupings of resting places. In their rush to out-surge each other, three of the youth lost their grasp of direction and landed in a tumbled mass against a slab of the stone wall that backed the circle. As they gathered their senses and laughingly gained their equilibrium, they all sensed movement. To their surprise, the slab of stone that they had run into began to tilt. It began by swinging open slightly, but then a cracking stone sound was heard and it slowly settled flat against the ocean floor.

The entire gathering of youth hovered nearby in amazement as this all happened. They were grateful that the stone slab had slowly opened and fallen. Had it happened fast while they were still in a tangle of disarray, they would certainly have been crushed to death. As the sand and sediment cleared, it was evident that they were looking into a large chamber. Two of the older youth were anxious to move forward and explore. But their companions, sensing danger, held them back. They realized that if one slab of stone fell, others could be unstable.

While the rest of the gathering stood by to stand guard, the two adventurist youth surged off to find elders to report to. In a short while Jennis and a delegation of elders approached. Examining the area and opening, they conferred among themselves. Jennis felt the stone wall on either side of the opening. He sensed that no more movement was happening. With permission of the elders, he carefully drifted up to and into the opening.

Everyone present hovered stone still, in fear of what might happen. After what seemed a very long while, Jennis reappeared. He shocked the entire Delmar gathering as they hovered in wait. His lower arms were encased in ornate gleaming shafts of metal. His magnificent muscular chest was heavily laden with circles that glowed with embedded shiny stones. To complete his shocking revelation, in each hand he carried dangerous looking but incredibly shiny articles that were obviously weapons.

Later that light, Jennis led the entire elders gathering through the previously hidden chamber. It was unanimously decided that this had to be the treasure chamber of the pillared one who's image stood at the entrance to this circle of pillars. He had to have been the leader of these dry place creatures.

Jennis was charged with the task of leading the Delmar protectors into the chamber in small groups to safely remove any weaponry that might assist them in safeguarding their resting place, as well as protecting the pillared ones from deep predators. In the chamber, Jennis also found several circles of shiny encrusted metal that they all now knew were head pieces for a ruler to wear.

There was enough treasure in the chamber for Jennis to make a proposal to the elders council. They agreed and gave him permission. For the next several lights, Jennis guided each adult Delmar male into the chamber. They each chose a shiny gift to give to their life and birth giving partners. Jennis chose bright encrusted circles to give to Bahari and the rest of his own intimate pod.

As the light filtered through the water on their next festival day it was quite a sight. Each and every Delmar present was adorned with a beautiful shiny article. Seeing this, the elders were concerned. They knew that in spite of the depth of the gathering, if a ray of light found its way deep enough, it might reflect off of one of the colorful stones that encrusted the shiny metals. They assigned pairs of watchers to hover near the surface to warn of approaching pillared ones crafts. It would have been devastating if a nearby surface craft or a pillared one peering into the depths from his or her floating structure spotted the gleam from below.

As the waters began to overheat the elders announced that all Delmar needed to prepare for their migration to the cooler place. Once again, the migration went without major incident. There was just the usual changing of course to cope with predators and pillared ones' activities.

Once settled in, Taras summoned Jennis for a consultation. She had given a lot of thought to his suggestion of a small festival to be put on for Delja and her extended pod. It was decided that Jennis should oversee organizing this, what she saw as being a dangerous event. It took several lights to arrange. Many Delmar that he approached were too terrified to partake in the exercise. Finally, he was able to gather ten brave breeding pairs. They also agreed to bring their older spawn along.

A joint gathering of the Delmar, with Jasper and Ennis from the dry place would be both exciting and fraught with unknown consequences. For this first experiment, Jennis chose from a delegation of the stronger males and females who had agreed to take part. They were all Delmar who were not presently caring for new spawn.

On the appointed light Delja, Zeeman and little Jasper followed up the shore to the meeting place. Jasper and Ennis were already there, uncovered and ready to greet their Delmar family. Delja wasted no time in having Ennis convey what was planned for the day. Jasper Sr. was a little scared, but he trusted Delja so he entered the water, then lifted Ennis in with him. Ennis immediately swam on his own into Delja's arms. She was overjoyed that he had gained such confidence in her element.

Seeing that all was good, Zeeman ducked below the waves and sounded the welcome. In short order, many heads appeared, surrounding the grouping. Delja one by one gave the sounds of every Delmar to Jasper. In turn each one embraced him in the usual intimate Delmar tradition.

The light progressed in grand fashion. The males and females took turns giving Ennis and little Jasper rides on their backs, circling the small floating craft. Ennis was kept busy answering questions from each Delmar present. Many had wondered so much all of their lives about the pillared ones. They had rehearsed questions about their life and how they lived in the dry places.

As a result of listening to these questions and answers, Delja learned much that she hadn't known. Jasper's birthing male had been a fisherman. He was lost in a raging sea when Jasper was still young. Jasper and little Ennis lived with Jasper's birthing female. She prepared nourishment and cared for them all.

It pleased Delja to learn that her pillared small one was being lovingly provided for. She also learned that for some strange reason, this female had two sounds. Ennis called this pillared female, Nan and Jasper called her Mom. This Delja found strange as the Delmar only used one sound to be known by.

As the light started to fade, it was time to end the gathering. One pair of Delmar, Arcelia and Cadao approached Delja with a request. Rather than a brief parting embrace, they both wanted to experience holding a pillared one intimately in their arms. Delja relayed, the request to Jasper via Ennis. Jasper was not sure, but he agreed knowing that Delja wished him only love.

The couple came forward. Arcelia grasped Jasper in her arms and Cadao enfolded Ennis in his muscular arms. Jasper's senses peaked as this beautiful full-breasted Delmar held him tight and ran her hands over the hair on his chest, then down to feel his legs and manhood.

After a few minutes they let go. Jasper was relieved; he thought that it was done. He was thankful that his body was immersed below the rippling waves. It made it easier to hide his now-fully-engorged manhood. But to his surprise, Arcelia then grasped Ennis and Cadao welded his body tight against Jasper in an intimate embrace. Not only did Cadao hold Jasper tight with one muscular arm, but he also explored his back and bottom with his free hand. Jasper gasped when the hand felt deep between his buttocks and then forged in between their bodies, to feel his manhood.

At first Jasper was shocked, but seeing the expression on Delja's face, he relaxed and placed his arms around the smiling but nervous Delmar male, putting him at ease. Delja moved in close, adding her arms to the huddle. She gave Jasper the sounds for Cadao and Arcelia.

Now with Delja near and encouraging him to relax, Jasper did something that he had not done since first meeting Zeeman. He left one arm snugly wrapped around Cadao's waist. Freeing up the other, he ran his fingers through Cadao's luxurious hair. It was exceptionally light in color with just a blush of red. Jasper marveled at the thickness and length. It flowed to well below Cadao's middle back.

As Jasper drew his hand away from the ends of the long hair, Cadao grasped his wrist. He drew it down and in between their embrace. Jasper was shocked when his hand was settled onto Cadao's manhood. At first he was not sure, horrified that Cadao was suggesting a sexual exchange. But then Cadao grasped his manhood. Looking into his face, Jasper realized what was happening. There was only happiness and smiles evident. The embracing of intimate appendages was just the Delmar way of cementing their special bond of friendship.

In conformation of this, Delja did as she had done when first introducing Zeeman to Jasper. She placed her hand on Cadao's hand as he grasped Jasper's manhood. Smiling she made sounds to Cadao that all was well. Then she reached her other hand down and added it to Jasper's hand as he gripped Cadao's hard breeding member. As he had learned before, Jasper knew that this was a bonding exercise to cement friendships and in no way contained an aspect of sexual aggression.

With the help of translations from Ennis, Jasper was grasping concepts and understanding more. The female that he loved along with their son and her pod was better evolved than his people. They were natural and openly intimate when it came to friendships, relationships and familiarity with each other's bodies.

Love for all creation flowed among these creatures. Unlike his fellow humans, Delmar love was all encompassing. Hatred and violence did not exist in their psyche. They barely had the ability to understand and cope with these horrible emotions when confronted by them from the pillared ones or deep water predators. Their existence was continually being challenged by both his people and the predators of the deep. He was now wishing that humans could share many of the heartfelt traditions and attitudes that these creatures of the deep believed in.

After a long pleasant interval everyone parted and Cadao helped Jasper lift the fast growing Ennis back into the floating craft. He then grasped Jasper in his massive muscled arms, hugged him tight and then lifted him bodily into the craft. Blushing, Jasper quickly helped Ennis fasten his lower covering then donned his own. As the steady breeze carried his craft away, he and Ennis waved towards all of their newly expanded Delmar family.

22

Reporting back to the elders, Jennis was pleased to relate how well the meeting went with Jasper and Ennis. Many of the elders were still afraid and cautious but hoped that this new communication would be good for their future safety.

For the next several cycles, the annual gathering with the pillared ones happened. More and more Delmar participated now that they felt safer around Jasper and Ennis. Delja was amazed every cycle by how much Ennis had grown.

One festival meeting proved to be extremely embarrassing for Ennis. He greeted his birth giver with his usual tenderness; as always she held him tight for a while. Jasper was also used to being held naked against men and women who felt naked on the top half and firm and scaly on the bottom.

That light Delja made a discovery. Since last cycle Ennis had sprouted a small growth of hair just above his mating organ. Ennis was not embarrassed when his mother examined and felt it. The embarrassment came when she made sounds for all who were present, drawing each and every one in to closely examine his adolescent development. Jasper was hovering nearby snugly supported above the waves, embraced in greeting between Zeeman and Cadao. He could not help but laugh. He told Ennis not to be embarrassed. He assured his son that they were not making fun of him. In fact they were excited for him that he was growing into an adult.

At each gathering, Jasper with Ennis translating, made a report to Jennis about the difficult struggle in trying to make the pillared ones aware of the poisoning of the water. The fact that by doing so they were destroying too many of the ocean's creatures only garnered empty words in response.

Jasper believed that the financial powers and politicians had in their mind that the oceans were strong and tolerant and would rebound from any attack. They believed that the growth of sea creatures needed to supply their needs would be never ending. The concept in their minds that entire species could become extinct did not in any way register. They looked solely at the magnificent sizes of the ever growing catches and the profits that they were bringing to market.

Having the seed of an idea, Jasper had Ennis ask Delja what this special day's festival was called. Over the years it had slowly grown, as more and more Delmar became brave enough to want to meet and explore the pillared members of Delja's intimate pod.

It was Ennis who finally found a name. Delja and Zeeman had difficulty at first, to form the complicated sounds, but loving

Ennis, they worked at it till they got it right. The festival would from now on be called 'Family Love Day'. Ever so slowly, Ennis was able to help Delja and Zeeman understand the meaning of the words 'family' and 'love' as well as the pillared sound for a light being a 'day' and a dark being a 'night'.

Finally, the cycle came when Ennis being fully grown almost the same size and physique as Jasper. Surprisingly, Ennis proved to have inherited another wonderful gift from his mother. He could spend the entire light cavorting in the waves with his ocean family and not be affected by immersion in the water. His skin, while not quite as firm as the Delmar males, could somehow withstand the softening effects of immersion. Jasper, on the other hand, was always quite shriveled and waterlogged by the end of every special family love gathering day.

On one such light the surface of the water was angry. It was threatening to develop into a raging sea. Ennis sounded to Delja that they could not stay long because of the fast approaching storm, but they would return in two days, once it passed.

Both Delja and Zeeman were amazed to learn that the pillared ones could now predict when a raging sea was going to happen and when it would end. That dark, Jennis shocked the entire Elders gathering with this revelation.

That cool cycle was a happy one for the Delmar community. The youth flourished and grew stronger. Thanks to a concerted effort by the Elders' council, the mating festival took place without major concerns. Bahari and Jennis were kept busy caring for their intimate pod, as well as completing tasks that the Elders' council requested.

During two times of raging waters, the Delmar witnessed crafts floundering against the shore. In both cases it happened near pillared ones gathering places. Help was immediately sent from the dry place to rescue the stranded. The Delmar rescuers kept watch to make sure, but they were not needed to bear up and save pillared victims.

It was easy for all to witness. As a result of the mating festival and continued partners rejoining, many Delmar female were fast approaching time to bring forth a new spawn. As the cooler cycle began to get uncomfortable for the Delmar, the elders announced that it was time to prepare for their migration to their warmer place. Two of the Delmar life givers had already brought forth a new life. It was dangerous for the pod to remain in the fast cooling waters any longer.

It took several lights to organize the entire gathering of intimate pods. Delja and Zeeman spent one last light in the loving embrace of Jasper and Ennis. Jasper surprised Delja with news. With Ennis translating, he explained that the cycle will come when they will also travel to the warm place in order to spend more time in the loving embrace of their Delmar family.

This news overjoyed Delja and Zeeman. Being most excited, Delja wanted to know how soon this would happen. Ennis translated Jasper's reply slowly into Delmar sounds. He sounded to Delja that his nan, Jasper's birth giver, was getting older now and was not at all well. They could not leave her alone to care for herself. They had to be constantly nearby. Sadly, Ennis told Delja that once his nan was gone, he and Jasper would be free to travel to the warm place.

Hearing this news, Delja and Zeeman gathered Jasper and Ennis in a loving embrace. Delja sounded that she had always been so grateful that Jasper's birth giver had loved and cared for Ennis so well over his many cycles. She expressed that she wished she could meet her and thank her for all that she had done for Jasper and Ennis

Ennis translated this to his father, then sounded to Delja. "We both wish that you could meet Nan. She is a wonderful loving person. She accepted me into her home and heart without judgment or question. But she does not know about our Delmar family. Dad decided early on when I was still a little baby that if nan knew about the Delmar, it would be all too easy for her to make a mistake and let it be known that my birth-giver was not a pillared one. The danger was too great. Dad would not take any chance that would expose the reality of the family that he loves."

This news made Delja and Zeeman sad, but they fully understood the danger of exposure to the pillared community. The council of elders were right to be concerned. Delja decided that she would report this news back to the council, along with her appreciation of how well they continually made concessions to their rules in order that she, Zeeman, and their entire Delmar pod could continue to remain an active and loving part of her pillared spawn's life.

Three lights later, the entire Delmar pod began their migration to the warm place. As always, this passage went slowly. It would have been dangerous to experience the coming forth of new spawn during such an epic journey.

The Delmar pod found their deep secluded lagoon of sunken dwellings as they had left them. All were relieved to see that nothing had been disturbed. It meant that their warm resting place continued to be unknown to the pillared ones. Jennis confirmed to the elders council, what the entire pod had deducted. He explored the treasure chamber and found each item still in the exact places where he had left them.

The elders immediately organized the rotation of defenders to stand guard over the entrance to their hidden lagoon. Within two lights, they also organized the watchers to monitor the pillared ones as they risked great danger by riding the crests and faces of the towering waters. When asked by the younger defenders, they admitted that the riding of the towering waters never ceased. But they also sounded to the youth that because the overheated waters would endanger their health and the health of the entire pod, they had no choice but to retreat to their cooler place lagoons when the waters in these parts overheated.

Along with the rising and lowering of the waters every light and dark, the Delmar's time in the warm place moved on. The protectors kept up their watch, but no threats were posed towards their resting place. This cycle, the dry places were filled even fuller with pillared ones enjoying the heated sand and water. Several episodes happened when deep predators had to be repelled so that the pillared ones could escape to the dry place while their protectors warded the predators off.

On one occasion, a male suffered an injury to one of his pillars when a deep predator grabbed him. Luckily, when this happened, he was closely surrounded by other pillared ones. They were all in the process of fleeing to safety. As the pillared one struggled against the pull of the predators strong grip, one of his pillared companions discharged an enormously loud instrument against the predator's side. It did not destroy the creature, but it did have the desired effect. The predator let go of the pillar and immediately surged away to safety.

Observing from the crest of distant swells, the Delmar protectors could see pillared males holding him up from both sides and helping the damaged male leave the water. The Delmar rescuers were happy to see that the pillared male would now be safe. Once the pillared ones had reached the safety of the dry place, other pillared ones awaited him with a carrying platform. They laid him down and rushed him away. The Delmar protectors assumed that, like themselves, pillared ones must have healers that administer to their injuries and illnesses.

23

The lights wore on and in time they began to lengthen. As they did, it was inevitable. The longer more intense lights caused the waters to get hotter. By the time the elders council announced that it was time to prepare to head to the cooler place, the entire pod was more than ready.

As much as they preferred their surroundings in this warm place, they all were infused with the excitement of the upcoming mating festivals. None were more excited than the coming-of-age youth. That feeling was also being felt by the older males and females, ones who were this cycle anticipating an intimate joining with their chosen mating partners in the deep lagoons. The excitement of mating after two full cycles of caring for a new spawn as well as abstaining made their feelings even more intense. It made the upcoming festival all the more exciting, knowing that the end result would, hopefully, be the bringing forth of a new Delmar spawn to love..

This migration, the currents and waters cooperated. The pod's transit to the cooler place went without serious difficulty. The entire pod was relieved that they only had to change direction twice to avoid the pillared ones' gathering fibers. Each time they had to change directions, the elders and adult Delmar worked together to keep the pod tightly together and keep all safe. In the process, they also made certain to watch out for their more adventurist older youth. None wanted to repeat the danger caused by their youth going close to the great gathering fibers.

That cooler cycle's gathering took Delja's intimate pod's relationships to another level. When they finally had their first reunion in the secluded cove, Ennis had news for Delja. He sounded to her that he had now finished his education. He suggested that he begin to record a story about her society, making it sound like it was just fiction from his imagination.

Jennis was not sure about this. Deep in conference, Ennis was finally able to convey his entire concept. The story would emphasize the horror that his people wrought against the waters surrounding their world. He would make it clear that this poisoning and destruction of the water creatures would in the end destroy humans along with the ocean's life.

Jennis finally agreed that it might work. He was terrified though. How would he tell the council of Elders that Ennis was recording aspects of their story. His only comfort was that he trusted Ennis. Ennis promised that he would not even hint that the Delmar actually existed. He would only refer generally to all the sea's inhabitants as 'Sea Creatures'.

During this cooler cycle, a new problem arose at the extended gathering of the Delmar and their pillared family. Ennis was now more than fully developed. He was actually bigger in size and muscle than Jasper. Delja was so proud of the beautiful creature that she had brought forth.

Because Ennis was still just in his late teens and knowing that Jasper Jr. was two cycles younger than him, he was unprepared for the shock of learning that Jasper Jr. was old enough to be allowed to mate. While he had certainly had forays into interaction with the opposite sex, the thought of choosing one to commit to forever was not something that he was prepared for. At his age and in his society, it was hardly acceptable to be intimate with the opposite sex, let alone for a teenager to choose and commit to permanence.

During the warm cycle that had passed, Delja and Zeeman's Jasper Jr. had come of Delmar age. As soon as they all met for a happy reunion, Jasper Jr. embraced his half brother Ennis, as they always did, but instead of letting go he opened one arm and gestured. In short order a beautiful young Delmar female came forward to be enveloped in their gathering. Ennis was amazed to learn that this female carried the sound Ephyra. She and Jasper had recently chosen each other to be a permanent mating pod.

Ennis had many cycles before been introduced to Jasper's male life partner, Llyr. On their first encounter, it was embarrassing and difficult to make Llyr understand that he could not intimately enter and possess Ennis. For the Delmar males, it was an accepted and sensually enjoyable way to bond.

Ennis was by now, quite used to having both play times and intimate discovery times with his Delmar sibling and his life partner. During one festival, Ennis actually relented and eased his rule. That light was an education for Ennis. He was entered by both his Delmar sibling and his life partner, Llyr. In return, he entered both Jasper Jr. and Llyr. Ennis had no desire to repeat this activity on future festival days, but he was happy that he did that one time. He now realized how important the intimate joining and bonding was in cementing close relationships for the Delmar.

Unknown to Ennis, Jasper senior, Delja and Zeeman had had to keep a close eye on him for several cycles now. At each gathering, more and more female Delmar were becoming brazen, attempting to explore what it would be like to be intimate with this most alluring young pillared one. Both Jasper and Delja knew from experience that this must not happen.

Ennis also knew by then, that when the day came and he chose a dry-place partner to mate with, it would be difficult. He would have to know that she understood who gave birth to him and accept that part of his life. He had been from birth completely comfortable totally uncovered and sharing tactile intimacy with his father, as well as the mature males, females and the Delmar youth that he played with on festival gatherings. A lifelong partner for Ennis would have to accept both the naturist aspect of his existence, as well as the unique intimacy of his extended Delmar family.

Ennis knew that his father had a duty to protect the Delmar and like his father, he also had a deep love for both Delja and Zeeman. Because of this bond and commitment, Jasper Sr. had never formed another lasting relationship, on the land. Ennis grew and flourished with his grandmother to love and nurture him. He never suffered for want of a mother on the land. He always knew that his mother beneath the waves was there and truly full of love for her pillared son.

Jasper Sr. was a tall, handsome man. There were many available females over the years who had tried to win his affections. He instinctively knew that none of them would be able to understand, nor accept, the intimate affection that he bore for his son and his Delmar family. It went too far beyond the norms of his culture to accept that level of intimacy as friendship and platonic love.

Jasper Sr., by choice, had remained alone. He cared for Ennis and his birth mother, who was now getting elderly and needing a great amount of his help. Ennis could see how the union between his father and Delja affected their lives. He hoped that some day in the not too distant future, he would meet that special one who could accept him as he was. He had discussed this many times with his father. They both held a deep-seated worry. Knowing who gave birth to him, Ennis worried that he carried enough genes in his body to cause his child to be born with the physical aspects of his Delmar birth-giver.

24

Two years after Ennis had met Jasper Junior's mating partner, Jasper senior and Ennis decided to undertake a journey south. Nan had died earlier that year. Jasper was now without the commitment to her care. He was now free to travel. Delja described the tall pillared resting places and the heavily populated sand beaches. She also sounded to Ennis about the rolling surf and the pillared ones riding the face of the giant water. With this information, Jasper was able to work out the location of the warmer place where the Delmar spent the colder part of their cycle, or as dry place creatures called it, 'winter'.

This location was the Delmar's new birthing home. It was not the place where Ennis would have come forth, had he arrived at the expected time. That place was lost to Delmar history because of the poisoned waters.

Traveling south by ship, Jasper Sr. and Ennis were surprised to find that it was in fact a heavily populated resort area. They wondered how the Delmar could exist in anonymity in such a place. As they had planned when last meeting with Delja, they bought a small floating craft that was propelled by a pole and a large cloth. Ennis had taught the Delmar that the sound for this craft was 'Sail boat" and that the cloth that gathered the wind to move it forward was called 'Sail'.

Their plan worked perfectly. They had but to sail back and forth out from the populated beaches but well beyond the surf line. On the second day, a delegation of Delmar watchers, led by Zeeman, located their craft. Jasper let out a long line from the bow and set the sail, keeping the rudder centered. Unknown to the humans nearby, a gathering of young Delmar males grasped the rope from below the surface and guided the craft away from the crowds.

To anyone on the shore or in the water it would have looked like the small sail boat was sailing further down the shore. Rounding several points, they were drawn into a secluded cove. It was completely walled in by high dangerous cliffs. There was a small sand beach, nestled at the deepest point of the cove. The entire inlet looked inaccessible and pristine. Jasper believed that their Delmar family had chosen well. They could be together in safety here.

For the next five lights, Jasper and Ennis spent their days in the lagoon. They so enjoyed being uncovered. After all of these years, Jasper felt completely happy and comfortable frolicking in the surf, experiencing the intimate physical contact that was natural to the Delmar. For Ennis, it was even more so. It was not a learned habit; it was all that he had known since he was born.

When they arrived at their secret cove on the sixth light, a surprise greeted them. Rounding the headland, they could see a wisp of smoke rising from the dry sand, just back of some large boulders. The Delmar had already observed this and were concerned. Ennis had the Delmar youth secure the long rope to a rock on the sandy bottom so that their craft would not drift away. Delja and Zeeman cautiously approached Jasper's craft. Jasper was never able to grasp any more than basic happy and heralding sounds that the Delmar used. Thanks to the translation skills of Ennis, he could, however, communicate.

It was decided that Jasper should investigate the source of the smoke. By then he was already in the water and as always, comfortable being without clothing. He swam ashore naked. Stepping from the water, Jasper carefully walked up to the large boulders. He attempted to discretely peer around one side of the bolder. To his surprise, a young woman was sitting on a blanket tending the small fire. In wonderment he realized that she was as naked as he was. He decided that the safest thing to do would be to retreat back to the water and report to the Delmar that the risk was not great.

Straightening and turning towards the water, Jasper stopped dead in his tracks. He was now standing face to face with a beautiful woman near his own age. The shocking fact was obvious. Like the young woman at the fire, this woman was also naked. She looked and sounded angry, accusing him of sneaking up and looking at her daughter's naked body.

Jasper begged forgiveness, "I promise that my intent was not to look at your daughter. I was only wondering how there could be a fire on such an inaccessible beach? I was concerned that it might be someone who was marooned and unable to escape this walled-in place. If that was the case, I have my boat and could rescue whoever was here."

The woman said, "It might be inaccessible to most, but not to us. My daughter and I live in that cottage at the top of the cliff. Over a hundred years ago the privateer who built our cottage took advantage of fissures deep in the cliff to build a stair down through the levels. We discovered it years ago when we first moved here. It took a long time for us to rebuild the old stair system. We wanted to keep it our secret. As you can see, we love the ocean and also love being without clothing. What we don't love is sharing our nakedness with the hoards of thrill-seeking riffraff who habituate the resorts and beaches down the way."

Jasper could certainly accept this. He also wanted nothing to do with the crowded beaches and mass nudity. He introduced himself and told the woman, "I agree with you completely. As much as I enjoy being naked, I would never go to a public nude beach. That is why I sought out this inaccessible cove. I have enjoyed the past five days here with my son, Ennis. He is swimming in the lagoon near our anchored craft."

Still a bit leery she introduced herself as Aaralyn and told Jasper that her daughter's name was Delphia. Sensing that there was more than what was obvious before her eyes, she suggested that at the end of the afternoon, Jasper bring his son and join them for some food by the fire. Jasper, for the first time in many years, felt a stirring in his loins as he stood naked before this beautiful woman. He was anxious to get back into the water before he became embarrassingly engorged. He asked if he could bring something to add to the meal. Aaralyn suggested that if he was also fishing, he might bring a fish to roast over the fire.

Jasper promised that he would bring a fish to roast, then bid farewell and quickly returned to the sea. He swam out to the boat and located Ennis who was cavorting with his half-brother Jasper and Llyr. As soon as he gathered them for a conference, Ennis, Jasper Jr. and Llyr all knew that something important had happened to Jasper. Each of the three reached below the surface and felt Jasper's stubbornly rigid mating organ. It certainly was not a unique event. Rigid organs were a daily part of all Delmar males' lives. When together playing in the water with their extended family, Jasper Sr. and Ennis also accepted their frequent erections as normal. But this light it was evident. There had been no intimate play time happening with Jasper Sr. to have created such a stubborn reaction that refused to fade away. All three youth sensed that something important had happened.

Delja and Zeeman soon appeared at the surface, concerned over what Jasper had found out on the dry place. Through Ennis, Jasper filled them in on what happened on the beach. Pointing upward towards the cliff top, Jasper indicated where the woman and her daughter lived. From where they floated in the center of the cove, only the upper walls and roof of the cottage were visible. It was decided that Jasper and Ennis should accept the invitation in order to discover if this pillared female and her spawn constituted a threat to their safety.

At the end of the afternoon, they bid farewell to their Delmar family and rowed the small craft towards the beach. Hauling the hull high and dry, Jasper was unsure if they should at least carry clothing up to the fire, in case their hosts were now covered. Rounding the boulder, it was evident. Neither woman had covered.

Aaralyn was surprised at the sight of them. She exclaimed, "When you told me that you had your son with you, I assumed that he was a young boy. You did not say that he was a grown man. Unsure what to answer, Jasper just replied, "You didn't ask how old he is."

Aaralyn just shrugged and went on with her meal preparation. Jasper presented his offering. It was a medium sized reddish fish. His namesake and Llyr had dived deep and captured it for him, just before they left for their own resting place. Settling on the far side of the now two blankets that covered the sand, Jasper thought it sweet that both Ennis and Delphia acted a bit shy, being newly introduced while naked.

25

By the end of the meal the mood had relaxed. Jasper could not remember ever feeling this good around any woman other than Delja. For the next two days, they rowed to the beach at the end of every afternoon to enjoy a meal and the company of their new friends.

As dark fell early during this time, Jasper Jr. and Llyr helped them out. They listened for Ennis to call them. When Jasper rowed the small boat out into the center of the lagoon, Ennis would lean over the side and immerse his face in the water. Then he echoed his calling sound into the depths. It never took more than a few minutes before Jasper Jr. and Llyr appeared. They grasped the trailing rope as Jasper Sr. lifted the sail. In the uneasy darkness, it could have been dangerous to navigate the on-shore currents under sail. Each time the young Delmar towed the boat back to within sight of the village where Jasper and Ennis were staying.

After their second evening on the beach with Aaralyn and Delphia, Jasper and Ennis talked deep into the night. Ennis had grown up as all Delmar male and female do, sleeping in the arms of their birth-givers.

This was a first conversation that Jasper and Ennis had ever had on this subject. As he held Ennis tight in his arms Jasper confessed to Ennis that for the first time since Ennis was born, that he had met a woman who excited his heart just as Delja had done in his youth.

Ennis confessed to his father that he had spurned many females in recent years, fearing they would not accept who and what he was. He told his father that, like his Delmar siblings, he would forever have the need to feel the safety and love of his life-givers embrace. This statement of enduring love opened Jasper's heart and he wept openly in Ennis's arms.

In the morning, they woke as always still cuddled tight together. Before they parted to begin their day, they talked further. Both agreed that they would let things ride on a day-to-day basis and try to gauge how open their new friends were. For the safety of their Delmar family, caution and extreme care was warranted.

That day, as before, they spent the afternoon cavorting in the lagoon with their Delmar family. That light, several young Delmar mating pairs brought their newborn spawn. Jasper and Ennis so loved when this happened. To cuddle and play with the bright eyed little ones was a pure joy.

It was always a new experience for father and son, when previously unknown Delmar greeted them. There was more often than not a certain amount of curiosity and exploring. After so many years, Ennis had taught Jasper the sounds for approval and restraint. When these young adults wanted to explore his form, Jasper could always set their minds at rest and utter the sound for approval. Likewise, when their curiosity came too close to intimacy, he was able sound that he was not comfortable. He did however learn to give this negative sound while smiling and tightening his embrace with the Delmar that was holding him. That way they knew that all was well and that he was just not available. It was completely beyond the Delmar's nature to force intimacy. It had to be a mutual desire.

The evening of the third day, Jasper and Ennis again joined their new friends for a meal on their secluded beach. As dusk was nearing, Aaralyn suggested a swim. Jasper was not sure, but Ennis was certainly enthused about the idea. They climbed into the small boat and Jasper rowed them to the center of the lagoon. He attached the anchor to the rope and gently lowered it over the side. If Aaralyn or Delphia noticed how gently Jasper lowered the weight to the sandy bottom, they didn't comment.

One by one, they jumped into the warm water. It was great fun to swim with their new friends. Just when Jasper was beginning to relax Delphia called out, "Mom, everyone get back into the boat fast; I think there are sharks here."

Just as the women were stroking towards the boat, two heads popped out of the water. Stunned, they stopped dead and trod water. Jasper swam around the boat to see what was there. Unsure of what to say, he decided the safest way to proceed would be to introduce the young men. He so hoped that they would not move around enough to make their lower half visible. He was also grateful that their ample heads of long flowing hair more than covered their vents.

Seeing this, Jasper spoke up right away, "Aaralyn and Delphia, I would like you to meet Ennis's half-brother Jasper Jr. and his close friend Llyr. We were not expecting them here today; it is a good surprise. Before she could speak, he added, "They can only make sounds and smile. They do not have the ability to speak." Ennis wasted no time in diving below the surface so as not to be observed and made sounds to communicate to the boys to be careful, keep their distance and try not to sound a lot.

The mood relaxed somewhat, and everyone swam around in the near dark. But Jasper Sr. was worried. He wanted to shorten this encounter before anything happened. Just as he was about to suggest they take the ladies back to the beach, the moon broke from behind the heavy cloud covering.

It all happened so fast. Jasper junior was just in the process of passing Delphia. The full moon in all its radiance totally caught his entire shape. She gasped and turned, lifting herself into the boat. She called to her mother to come at once.

Once they were all settled back in the boat, Jasper knew that something was wrong. As he rowed back to the beach he got up enough nerve, "Delphia, I can tell that you are upset. I promise you there is nothing to be afraid of. If you want to talk about it, I'll help you understand what you saw." To a surprised Aaralyn, Delphia looked right at Jasper and asked, "What are you and what are they?"

Jasper felt trapped, thinking If he told them and they didn't handle it well, who would believe them if they told others? They're two women who shun society and live a hermit life. He confessed,

"They are what I said, Ennis's half-brother and his companion. I know that you saw, so I will not try and lie to you. They are not of us. They are called Delmar. They live below the ocean waves.

This statement made both ladies gasp in horror. Jasper quickly continued in hopes of calming them. "Many years ago I met Delja, Ennis's mother while out on the ocean, fishing. We fell in love and spent an entire summer together making love in the surf. When she gave birth, we expected the baby to be like her. Instead, we were both surprised when Ennis was born. He was physically like me, so unable to live beneath the waves. Since then, we have become an intimate part of Delja's extended family. We are usually only together in the summer, up North near where we live. This is the first time that we've traveled to their warm season place."

Taking this in, Aaralyn asked, "So you're telling me that they are your family, and they wish us no harm?"

Jasper assured her, "I promise you, harm is not within their culture. They are extremely intimate, well beyond our norms. As Ennis has grown, I have learned to accept the sensations of close physical contact with him and our Delmar family. It is evident by his nakedness, Ennis is a handsome boy with every part in place that a boy his age should have. What we do not know, and have no way of telling, is the future. If he ever procreated, we could only wonder if any of his mother's genes would affect his offspring."

Jasper decided that as he had gone this far, he might as well continue. For better or worse, his fast growing feelings for Aaralyn gave him the courage to chance everything. Looking at Aaralyn, he told her, "I would like you to meet Delja, her mating male Zeeman and our entire extended family, but I must have their permission first. They do not harbor hatred for any living creature, but they fear many. Sharks and other ocean predators often prey upon them. They also suffer at our hands. The intolerance and hatred of man continually ravishes the fish stocks in the ocean depths and at the same time poisons its waters.

"They use, as an example, the plight of the whales. The whale community lived in peace, wishing harm to no one and yet man slaughtered them mercilessly. The Delmar fear such a slaughter if they became known. In their non-aggressive minds, they believe that the whales were slaughtered because of our hatred. They have no concept that we boiled them down and used them to light our lamps. Even so they could never accept the killing of kind gentle creatures, just to have a lamp lit.

Hearing all of this, Delphia whispered into her mother's ear. With a surprised look on her face she asked Jasper, "My daughter wants me to invite you and Ennis up to our home tonight. We can secure your boat on the beach. There is little tide here and no storms predicted."

That night was a milestone in both their lives. Jasper Sr. lay with a woman of his own kind for the first time in his life. As a young man, he had been a virgin when Delja enchanted him into her arms. Ennis had thought all along that his first intimate sexual experience would be with a male or female or both at once, but definitely a Delmar. Ennis had not considered that one occasion, when he shared intimately with his half-brother and Llyr, was actually sex. He was amazed to sleep in the arms of Delphia after an exhausting session that amply destroyed his virginity.

Two afternoons later, Jasper and Ennis anchored in the lagoon and entered the water. In short order, Jasper and Llyr appeared. They asked their Delmar family to seek out Delja, Zeeman and Jennis. Once they were all together, they had a lengthy conference, using Ennis to translate.

Jennis was very protective of his community. In the end he agreed to have a limited gathering for these new pillared ones, but he warned Jasper. If they bring on danger and suffering for his people, he would not hesitate to destroy them just as he destroys the deep predators when they attack the Delmar.

Jasper and Ennis assured Jennis that they agreed and believed that all would be well. They promised to back up Jennis with their own support if things went badly.

The following afternoon, the small boat was rowed to the center of the lagoon and carefully anchored. Once they were all naked and in the water, heads started to appear. First, they met and embraced Ennis's mother Delja and her partner Zeeman. Next, they met Jasper's namesake and both his life and mating partners.

Aaralyn and Delphia had been amazed as they rowed out to the center of the lagoon. Listening to Ennis explained how the Delmar society lived left them in awe. They looked unsure, so Jasper Sr. decided that a demonstration was in order. He talked to Ennis who began making sounds. In no time, Ennis was held intimately and tight from front and back by his Delmar brother and his life partner Llyr.

At the same time Zeeman and Cadao came forward, tenderly embracing Jasper. To everyone's surprise suddenly Delja and Arcelia surfaced and gathered Aaralyn and Delphia into their arms.

All the Delmar in unison began to swirl in circles and chant their happy sounds.

Once this demonstration was over, everyone moved about. It was an intimate show and tell experience that Aaralyn and Delphia would never forget. The highlight of the afternoon for Aaralyn and Delphia was when two mating pairs of Delmar surfaced with their newborns in arms. They were afraid but Ennis sounded to them that it was safe. Each pair approached the women and after an intimate embrace they allowed a totally amazed mother and daughter to cradle and play with the tiny Delmar spawn.

By the end of the light, the Delmar sadly parted from their new friends. For the next few weeks, Jasper and Ennis spent their days frolicking with their Delmar family, and their nights, in the passionate arms of their new loves. By the time their return north to their home was due, they had formulated a plan.

Jasper had lost his elderly mother the previous year. He had no ties keeping him in the northern waters. With the agreement of Aaralyn and Delphia, they returned home and disposed of their house and most of their belongings.

26

Three months later they were ensconced with Aaralyn and Delphia in the cliff-top cottage. It was a large rural property, well away from the commercial part of the shoreline.

The cottage only had two small bedrooms. Jasper and Aaralyn decided that Ennis and Delphia should have their own home. Plans were made to build a suitable cottage for a young couple. It was a great bonding experience for them all. Jasper and Ennis worked themselves to exhaustion moving rocks and cementing them in place to form the foundation and outer walls. Once they began woodworking and finishing Aaralyn and Delphia worked tirelessly to assist through every step of the construction.

At least once a week, on the calmest day, all four took the small boat, rowed out to the center of the lagoon and anchored. Ennis was always the first to shed his clothing and enter the water. While the rest were removing their coverings, he would dive below the surface and let go with a loud vibrating sound. Everyone in the boat was barely aware that he made a sound, but it echoed through the depths to reach their Delmar family. On every occasion, at least some Delmar came forth to socialize. Some days it was a mixture of adults and youth. Other days it was just the youth who were free to play.

After a month, finally one day, Delja and Zeeman appeared. Zeeman spent time having an intimate swim with Jasper, while Delja cavorted with Aaralyn and Delphia. They were also now comfortable with the intimate tactile ways of the Delmar. While this was happening, Ennis could be seen floating off to one side of the boat deep in communication with Delja.

That evening, sitting by the fire in the clifftop cabin, Ennis had an announcement to make. Kneeling on one knee, he first asked Aaralyn if she would marry him. While continuing to hold Aaralyn's hand, he then turned to Delphia. Grasping her hand, he asked her if she would marry his father. Both women, laughing at the strange proposal, chanted in unison, "Yes.

Jasper was both totally shocked and overjoyed by this event, and then amazed when Ennis announced that the rings he ordered would be delivered in three days. This puzzled Jasper. He well knew that Ennis had not been to the populated tourist center and had no actual money at his disposal.

Three days later, Ennis requested that only he and Jasper go out in the lagoon to meet their Delmar family. Jasper was at a loss for the reason. But he complied. Once they were anchored and naked, father and son slipped side by side into the warm water. Ennis put his face into the water and let go with a loud vibration.

Being in the water immediately by his side, Jasper felt the sound waves pass right through his body. He was amazed as he had never before been close enough to the source to feel the vibrations of the communication calling.

In just a few minutes, two heads appeared. It was Delja and Zeeman. As was tradition, they all shared intimate embraces and greetings. Ennis then told Jasper, "Mother offered to help when I explained to her the tradition of giving a ring to one's intended. Actually, in the Delmar society, they also give a special gift when they are beginning the mating part of their development."

Puzzled, Jasper asked, "I understand the concept of giving. But what I don't understand is how can your mother be of help in getting us rings?"

Ennis just smiled and gestured out towards the open water. He told his father, "You will see in a few minutes." Looking around, Jasper realized that Zeeman had disappeared. In no time at all he reappeared. Surging to the side of the boat Zeeman reached out of the water and deposited a large bundle of seaweed on the floor of the hull. Ennis enveloped a smiling Zeeman in his arms and made sounds of happiness.

Jasper had so far been unable to learn what each sound meant, but over the years he had learned to differentiate between sounds of happiness, sorrow and concern. He had also learned that the Delmar didn't have a sound for anger or hatred in any of its forms. Jasper could tell for certain that these were extremely happy sounds. In response to this, Delja drew into Jasper's arms, smiling widely. She reached out to Ennis and Zeeman who joined them in a family group huddle.

After a while Jasper and Ennis gave both Delja and Zeeman farewell embraces. They climbed back into the small boat and rowed to shore. Once it was secured, high up on the beach, Ennis motioned to Jasper to see what he had. Carefully unwrapping the woven seaweed parcel, Ennis and Jasper gasped. Spread out before them was a collection of jewel-encrusted rings and necklaces. Ennis proudly told his dad, "Mom knew where to find these, deep below the waves. They are from old galleons that sank many hundreds of years ago."

While being awed, Jasper was immediately aware of impending danger. He made a decision, telling Ennis, "We will go to the town and purchase two basic gold wedding bands. They will be the rings that our wives will wear in public. These rings and necklaces can be worn by our wives for their personal pleasure. But they can only wear them in the privacy of our home. These jewels can never be seen in public."

He reminded Ennis, "We are just poor common folk. If it were known that we had such jewels, we would be at risk of being robbed and possibly killed for them. If the wrong people heard of us owning such treasure, it could put our lives and the Delmar in jeopardy. They would uncover too many truths while forcing us to reveal where this came from. These can't be singular pieces; they must be part of a much larger trove of treasure."

Ennis was surprised by all this. He had not thought of the dangers when he asked his mother for help. But hearing what his father said made sense. He agreed, "Dad, you are right. Mom told me that it is a large old wooden craft that sank a long time ago. She told me that it is laden with shiny treasure. She offered to bring up as much as we needed. I never thought about it being a danger for us or the Delmar. I must tell Mom as soon as I can see her."

Jasper decided, "We should be able to create a safe hiding place deep in the fissure area of the rock face. The day may come when we need money. We could sell a ring or a stone to a jeweler, but not to one near here who knows us."

That evening they unwrapped an old piece of sail from around the jewels and rings to show their intended. For a while Aaralyn and Delphia just stared in shock at the treasure, then gingerly picked up and examined it piece by piece. In the end, each chose a ring to be their special one. Jasper and Ennis also chose rings to celebrate their union.

The following day, all four worked in a landing area in the rock fissure, halfway between the beach and the basement of the house. A safe hiding place was created and disguised in case anyone ever stumbled onto the stairway from the beach. The upper entrance from the house was well hidden by a trap door in the cold cellar.

Three days later, when they took a watery break, Delja and Zeeman appeared. Aaralyn and Delphia were now used to their Delmar ways, and tightly embraced Delja and Zeeman in thanks for the beautiful gifts.

27

By the end of the warm season, the new cottage was ready. Jasper went to town and arranged for the minister to pay a visit. Ennis had first wanted the ceremony to take place on the beach so that his Delmar family could observe from the surface of the lagoon. Jasper reminded Ennis that to do this would mean exposing the minister to the fact that they had a secret staircase to the sand below. There would also be great danger so close to the water's edge. That would bring their Delmar family into full view. Ennis agreed that in his enthusiasm he had forgotten about safety.

A compromise was worked out. They positioned the minister very near the edge of the cliff, with his side to the water. Thanks to their superior strength of vision, their entire Delmar family could witness the ceremony. With his side to the water, there would be no chance of his witnessing the large number of objects floating on the surface of the lagoon. It all went smoothly. He performed a double ceremony. Each couple stood as witness for the other. A special seafood feast was enjoyed that evening. The ocean delicacies were all provided by Ennis's mother and Zeeman.

The following day they all went to the lagoon. To their surprise, Delja and Zeeman brought over thirty of their Delmar family to greet and welcome the newlyweds. Many of the Delmar pod who had previously met Aaralyn and Delphia brought pieces of treasure as celebration gifts. A fun and exhausting day was had by all. When the wedding party returned to the beach, they secured their wedding gifts alongside the original treasure trove.

That evening Delphia had a surprise for everyone. "I've heard from my brother Galon. He is a dive instructor in Vancouver. He was unable to arrange the time off to be here for our wedding, but he will be here soon. Galon will visit us in two weeks. I have asked him to bring his dive gear. We can rent tanks for him and additional gear for all of us. He will give us all dive instructions. By next season we will have a surprise waiting for our Delmar family. We'll meet up with them in their environment, below the waves." Jasper and Ennis thought that this was a grand idea.

While planning for their visitor, Jasper and Aaralyn had to make a decision. Both agreed that at this point it was too soon to and too dangerous to make Galon aware of their Delmar family. They both agreed that in time this could happen.

Before Galon's arrival, Ennis spent time in conference with Jennis and his Delmar family. Jennis would make certain that all Delmar stayed away from their lagoon for the two weeks of Galon's visit. Jasper hoped that no Delmar would be overtaken by curiosity.

If they were, not only would Galon be made aware that the Delmar existed; the surprise of them all learning to scuba would be lost.

The scuba lessens went well. Galon was not licensed to issue certificates where they lived. He went into town and showed his credentials to the local dive instructors. It was agreed. Before he flew home, he would bring them all in for three lessons in order to pass their shallow water dive test and be certified. The evening before he left, Aaralyn cooked a great seafood feast on the beach. Once again Delja and Zeeman had provided the delicacies from the deeps.

That morning Galon had gone to town on his own. He returned with bottles of wine and champagne. After the meal, Galon stood and made a toast. He told everyone, "I want to thank you all for making this vacation so very special. I am pleased to know and already love my new family members. Because Aaralyn and Delphia are my only family, I have missed being near them since they chose to live here.

"Today that changed. The dive shop in town has offered me a partnership. The increased numbers of tourists have taxed them beyond their physical and financial capacity. I will either wind down or sell my operation in Vancouver and ship my equipment here. There is a shortage of instructors here, so I will bring as many of my crew who wish to relocate to a twelve month summer climate. I do look forward to that. Back home we have to use an indoor pool for half of the year. It is just not a natural place to work in for a deep sea diver. It will take a few months for it all of this to come together, but we will soon be one big family. I plan to rent a small space to stay in town to start. I will need to organize the expanded shop and get familiar with the local businesses. But in the end, I could not be happier, if my dear sister and her husband would allow me to build a cottage on this amazing property."

After his announcement, everyone rush to hug and kiss him. It all happened before anyone gave it a thought. Galon was a little startled when Jasper and Ennis took their turn, held him bodily tight and gave him what he thought was a passionate kiss. Witnessing this and Galon's reaction, Aaralyn and Delphia broke into peals of laughter, then returned to Galon's side and gave him the same 'Delmar style' greeting of happiness.

To the shocked look on Galon's face, Aaralyn told her brother, "We have different customs here. You will get used to it. I promise that I will explain it all once you are living among us. Just be assured that when we or our spouses bodily embrace and kiss you in our customary local way, we are expressing our platonic love for you. It is in no way a suggestion of wanton sexuality." Relieved at hearing this, Galon opened the bottles of champagne so that they could all celebrate his news.

The day after Galon flew back home, everyone piled into the boat and rowed to the center of the lagoon. Ennis was anxious to see his family once more. He knew that the weather was beginning to heat up. After conferring with Delja and Zeeman, Ennis announced that the pod was preparing to head north to their breeding festival place. Jasper remembered it fondly. It was Ennis' birthing home and the place where he met Delja and created his beloved Ennis. It was also where he grew up, and where his mother and father were laid to rest. Four days later, a final afternoon was enjoyed by Jasper,

Ennis, Aaralyn and Delphia in the lagoon while bidding farewell to all their Delmar family.

For the first time in a long while, Arcelia and Cadao were present. As soon as they recognized them, Ennis and Jasper explained to their wives the situation. They already knew and were used to the tactile intimacy that the Delmar enjoyed as part of their communication. But they were not aware of the intimate curiosity of this Delmar pair.

They were surprised when Jasper explained about this particular couple. He told the ladies, "Arcelia and Cadao are more tactile than most Delmar. They not only enjoy greeting bodily tight, but they also have a deep curiosity. It is not sexual, although to us, at first, it feels that way. They are simply curious about every aspect of our beings. That translates into the fact that when they hold you in a greeting embrace as all the Delmar do, they go further. They also freely caress your entire body, exploring its features and shapes.

"The first time that Cadao felt my intimate places, I was surprised, but I instantly realized that he was just being friendly and curious. When he realized that I was uneasy with him exploring the shape of my sex organ, he smiled and in exchange withdrew his organ from its folds and placed it in my hand. That's when I knew that it was just a continuance of their intimate friendship customs."

"So please relax and if they embrace you, be prepared for some hands exploring your shape. The Delmar are especially fascinated with our legs and how they're attached to our bodies. I have had to lift my legs up and down and flex my knees and ankles countless times, while curious Delmar grasped my hips, thighs, knees and ankles, in order to feel and visualize the bone structure and joint mechanisms that hold me upright. While their upper half has a bone structure exactly like ours, their lower half consists solely of tissue, massive amounts of muscles, and as you know, a covering of scales.

"They never seem to tire of watching us wiggle our toes; they actually think that it is a hilarious trick that we devised just to entertain the little Delmar spawn. I have never been able to convince them otherwise. The concept that we use our toes as an assist in balancing our movements doesn't seem real to them. Ennis assures me that to the Delmar, it's a total mystery how these leg appendages are able to hold us up to balance and carry us around what they call "The dry places. They also are amazed by the way the surfers are able to stand and use their legs to maneuver their boards on the crest and inner face of the great waves. I can only imagine how their minds would be blown if they could ever witness a live ballet performance.

"Oh yes, while we may call the Delmar Mermen and Mermaids or various versions of this, they have one major and one minor name for our kind. We are called 'The Pillared Ones', meaning our legs resemble the marble pillars of the sunken ruins. Their secondary name for us is "Flesh Creatures" because we are completely covered with soft flesh. As you already know, Ennis's flesh has a stronger resistance to the water than we all have. We tend to look like waterlogged prunes at the end of an afternoon in the lagoon. Ennis just glows with firm skin. His resilient skin and his ability to communicate with the Delmar are both a birth gift from his mother. We won't know if his body contains any further Delmar gifts until the day comes that he and Delphia have a child."

28

Six months later it became obvious that Ennis and Delphia had a new life on the way. Aaralyn decided that as long as Delphia didn't display any unusual signs that warranted medical attention it would be simple. She planned to deliver the baby. She had assisted several friends in the past with the birthing process. To be sure, she took Delphia to a clinic to have her condition assessed. Everything tested well through the nine months. The clinic knew from the start that it would be a home delivery. They made Aaralyn take a course to be certain that she knew how to proceed with the birth and what steps to take in calling for medical assistance should problems arise.

In early fall the time came. The overheated season was just ending. Not being sure what they were giving birth to, Ennis was anxious to have his mother nearby. Delphia had refused an ultrasound. She told the clinic that as long as there were no complications leading up to her delivery, she and her husband believed in being surprised when the birth happened. Every time she made this statement to another health care worker, Delphia would look at Jasper or her mother and smile widely, as she could see that they were also on the verge of nervous laughter.

On the night that Delphia went into labor, everyone was ready. Beyond the usual preparations to care for a newborn, they had done more. At the foot of Delphia's bed, Jasper had rigged a large copper lined crate that he filled with water. He had it heated to a comfortable temperature. When the time came close, Aaralyn and Ennis assisted Delphia to slip into the warm bath. It seemed to ease her contractions to have her body submerged. As the moment of birth approached, everyone held their breath in anticipation. Slowly a head appeared, then shoulders and chest. To a wide-eyed audience, in minutes, a beautiful well-formed boy slid from his mother's womb.

He was cradled in Aaralyn's hands while Delphia caught her breath. As she reached forward to gather her little son into her breast he gurgled and wiggled free of Aaralyn's grasp. To everyone's surprise, he looked around then started to clumsily swim towards his mother's breasts. Everyone was in shock. He was born with Delmar vision.

Jasper remembered at that moment that Ennis also had clear vision as well as the ability to more or less swim at almost the moment that he slipped from Delja's womb. It had been so many years since Jasper had seen that, he had forgotten this fact. As the new little one attached to Delphia's breast for his first feeding, Ennis slipped from his clothing and slid into the warm water in order to cradle his wife and new son in his arms. Jasper and Aaralyn watched the loving scene, weeping tears of joy, as they held each other tightly.

As Delphia and Ennis cuddled their baby and cooed over him, Aaralyn and Jasper discretely examined every inch of him. To their relief, there was no other signs visibly displayed that he had Delmar genes. They both knew that only time would tell. Ennis hoped that his little son would at least have the skill to communicate with his Delmar family. It would not take long before that was evident, to him at least.

Ennis and Delphia took a while to come up with a name for their son. She wanted to call him Jasper after his grandfather, but Ennis reminded her that there was already two Jaspers in their extended family, his dad and his half-brother. In the end they decided on a double name, He would be called 'Ronin Jasper'. Ronin had been the name of Aralyn's father. He was a career soldier who died in action.

Two months later, Ennis knew that it was time. For two days now, he had been feeling the water-born vibrations. Their entire family went down to the beach and launched the little boat. Once in the center of the lagoon, Jasper gently lowered the anchor to the floor of the lagoon. He no longer had the need to do this discreetly. Their wives now knew that it was to avoid hurting any family or sea life that might be below their craft.

Ennis was, as always, the first to disrobe and slide into the water. He dove below the surface and sounded his call. By the time that everyone but Delphia and little Ronin were floating on the glassy surface, two heads appeared.

To Ennis's delight it was Delja and Zeeman. Delphia beckoned them to the side of the boat. Reaching in, Ennis gathered a now naked Ronin into his arms and placed their son in Delja's arms. Gazing at the child, she sounded happy sounds as she wept with joy. In response, baby Ronin attempted to mimic her sounds. With wide eyes and wonderment, Ennis announced, "Ronin has inherited my ability to understand and communicate with our Delmar family."

As quickly as he announced this news, he was again amazed. Ronin wiggled free of his grandmother's arms and started with awkward motions to swim around her while gurgling and smiling. He was obviously like his father and grandfather, totally at home upon the waves. Witnessing this, Jasper and Ennis hoped that Ronin also had flesh, that like his father's could withstand the effects of long term immersion in sea water.

The next surprise was fast coming. Zeeman beckoned Ennis to his side. He gathered Ennis into his arms and grasped him tight. He then immediately began to swirl in circles while loudly sounding great expressions of happiness. As he had since he was little, Ennis enjoyed the sensations of being held tight while being twirled in the water by Zeeman's magnificent strength.

Zeeman was being so vocal that Ennis was unable to grasp the meaning of his ecstatic happiness. As the dizzying swirl continued, Zeeman shifted over to Delja's side. He then stopped the movement and reached for Ennis's hand. He then stretched it forward and settled it gently on Delja's very rounded belly.

Wide eyed, Ennis happily exclaimed for all to hear, "I'm going to have a new brother or sister."

29

Little Ronin was a delight to his parents and grandparents. He flourished and grew, thanks to the life giving nectar from Delphia's breasts. On a regular basis, Ennis and Delphia took Ronin in the boat to the center of the lagoon so that he could enjoy being in the water with his Delmar family. Jasper rigged a canvas awning that attached to the mast so that there would be protective shade for Ronin and Delphia. Jasper decided that a small cabin motor boat would be a better option for their growing family. He began to look around for one that would be light enough to haul up the beach on a hand hold carriage.

One month later Zeeman appeared in the lagoon alone. At first Ennis was concerned, but as soon as he was near, he grabbed Ennis, held him bodily tight and began his happy sounds as he swirled around. Ennis was greatly relieved. In short order, Zeeman sounded to Ennis that Delja had brought forth a female Delmar. He sounded that it had just happened and it had been difficult for her, so Delja was ordered by the healers to rest for a few lights before she brought her tiny spawn to the surface to meet her extended pod. He did have a message for Ennis; he sounded a request. He wanted Ennis to ask his mating partner if she would allow the new little spawn to carry her sound. Ennis assured Zeeman that Delphia would be proud to have the new Delmar spawn carry her sound.

Ennis waited till that evening to share his news. Like most days that they spent on the lagoon, they made a small fire and shared a meal in their private place behind the rocks on their beach. As they finished eating, Ennis went into the rock fissure and brought back a bottle of wine and glasses. He opened the bottle and poured everyone a glass. Raising his, he made an announcement. "You all saw me with Zeeman today. He brought me news. I now have a little sister. We will see her soon. She just arrived yesterday, so Delja is resting by order of the healers. The best part is, Zeeman asked for permission to give the little one Delphia's sound." Wide eyed at this announcement, Delphia jumped to her feet and yelled, "YES! I now have my very first goddaughter."

Six months later Galon arrived. The Delmar pod had already left for their cooler place. There would not be a need to enlighten him about the Delmar for a few months. Delphia remained home to care for Ronin. Ennis, Jasper and Aaralyn commuted to town to help set up Galon's tiny efficiency unit. Ennis and Jasper also helped Galon and his business partner to redecorate and organize their now expanded business space. They had taken over a closed shop that was right next door. With his family helping, none of the diving crew had to be pulled from their tight schedule to help out. Galon only brought two of his instructors with him. The rest chose to remain in Vancouver because of family ties.

Galon offered to have Ennis and Jasper certified as dive instructors. They declined and assured him that they would help in any other way possible. Galon was a bit puzzled, especially in the case of Ennis. He was a natural; totally at home in the water. Jasper had to take him aside and explain. He told Galon, "No one loves being in the ocean more than Ennis. But he has his reasons why he can't commit to doing it full time. He will share his reason with you soon, but the time is not right. You might even convince him, in time to be certified, so he could help out in the busy season with your beginners classes.

"Just be assured, we are all so happy to have you nearby at last, and we all want to support you in your business venture." Jasper had something to add, "Your sister and I are not in any way wealthy, but we are doing OK. If you have any financial needs, please don't hesitate to ask and we will do what we can to help out."

Galon assured Jasper, "I owned the small seaside shop in Vancouver that I used as a dive center. I bought it years ago when my father was alive, he helped me get started. Back then it was worth a fraction of what it's value is now. That is part of what fueled my decision to move. I had been holding off an amazing offer. Developers were buying up the small beachfront businesses in the hopes of building a luxury condo development. I was one of the last hold-outs. So, needless to say, the stakes were high to get hold of my little patch of land. Thank you for the offer, and if I am ever in need, I promise that I will come to you and Aaralyn first."

Back at home that evening, they had a long talk. It would not be that long before their Delmar family returned. The hyper-heat was already showing signs of letting up, With the more moderate warm temperatures, the hordes of snow-birds would start to arrive in an effort to escape the northern winter. Everyone was in agreement that they needed to be kept informed of where Galon would operate his classes. Their Delmar family must be given advance warning to stay away from that immediate area.

The newly revamped dive shop proved to be a going concern. Aaralyn could not help herself. She soon got involved in working in the shop. At her insistence they took one third of the retail area and turned it into a swim-wear boutique. Local tailors and seamstresses were more than glad to have a showcase for their custom-designed bathing suits and beach wear. Being an international Mediterranean location, Aaralyn had to stock what she thought was ridiculous, baggy North American style board shorts, along with the more popular mini speedo, bikini and thong styles for both men and women.

It took some doing but finally she was able to convince Galon that he would be more comfortable and of course hotter looking if he joined the local divers on his team and also wore slim speedo's to conduct his classes. She told him, "In a speedo, you look like a real international man. In those horrid baggy pool pants you look like an uptight shy north American. So I suggest you get with the program and blend in with the international scene here. After all, it's good for business."

The water was too warm in their region to warrant the wearing of rubber suits. Galon was a handsome muscular man. In no time he had to confess to his sister that he was being overwhelmed by sexual advances from both men and women.

Aaralyn shocked her brother by telling him, "Well, be it a man or a woman, if the timing is right and it feels good, go for it. Just enjoy the moment." There was a motive behind what she told her brother. She thought, 'If he doesn't get upset about that suggestion, it means he has an open mind. He will certainly need it when he meets my in-laws, not to mention when he first encounters Arcelia and Cadao'.

Shortly after that talk, their Delmar family returned. Jasper and Ennis had gone swimming every afternoon for a week in anticipation of having them answer Ennis's call. When finally Zeeman appeared to see who was there, the three gathered in a welcoming embrace. Ennis sounded to Zeeman that the next light, he, Jasper and Aaralyn would be in the cove to greet their Delmar family. He sounded to Zeeman that they had a surprise for Delja.

The following day they were ready. Once their boat was anchored in the cove, they all stripped naked, then donned their dive gear. That part of the cove was just under one hundred feet deep, well within their safety range. Once everyone was in the water, Ennis put his face below the surface and sounded his call to the Delmar. He then donned his face mask and mouth piece, then dove down to join Aaralyn and Jasper.

A short while after, it was evident that something was slowly approaching. It was Delja and Zeeman, followed by several of their Delmar family. It was obvious that they were being cautious. To set them at ease, Ennis removed his face mask and air hose and sounded to them that all was well. Now realizing who it was, Delja and

Zeeman surged forward to embrace their loved ones. An amazing afternoon was had by all. They circled and played beneath the waves. Ennis had to continually remove his mouthpiece to communicate. He realized that he needed to purchase a full face shield so that his mouth could be free behind the glass. He could then sound loud enough to communicate thanks to the Delmar's enhanced senses.

He sounded to Delja and Zeeman that, on occasion, Aaralyn would stay on the dry place to care for Ronin so that Delphia could join them for a day beneath the waves. Delja was disappointed. She sounded to Ennis, wondering why Ronin could not also be with them. After all, her little spawn and many other tiny Delmar were always with them.

It was difficult but Ennis explained that little pillared ones are unable to learn how to use the breathing equipment. That is why there was no small device made that would fit them. He promised Delja that as soon as Ronin was grown enough, he would have him trained and equipped so that he could dive below the waves with them. Meanwhile, he sounded that on a regular basis, they would all come to the cove for a day on the surface, like they had always done. This news made Delja and Zeeman happy and they hugged everyone tight as they swirled and echoed happy sounds. It was a revelation for Aaralyn and Jasper to hear the Delmar sounds actually vibrating through their bodies for the first time, below the waves.

30

One month later everyone decided that it was time to educate Galon. They decided on a plan. Three days later Galon had an afternoon off. When he arrived at the cottage, Aaralyn and Delphia were prepping the evening meal to be cooked in the fire pit on the beach. They told Galon that Ennis and Jasper were down at the beach laying a fire for later on. When he reached the foot of the staircase, Galon first saw the fire pit resting with kindling in place and a small pile of wood set off to a side. Nearby Jasper had erected a shade awning with lawn chairs nestled on the land side of the giant rock.

Galon then spotted Jasper and Ennis playing in the surf. As fast as they spotted him, they rushed out of the water. Galen was somewhat surprised when he saw that they were swimming naked. Jasper told him, "We have no need for modesty here, it's totally private. Actually the first time that Ennis and I encountered Aaralyn and Delphia here, we were all naked. The water is great; chuck your inhibitions and join us."

Galon hesitated for a moment, then shrugged his shoulders and stepped out of his sandals, T shirt and shorts. Witnessing this, Jasper thought, 'So far, our plan is working'. A few minutes later when they were playing three-way catch with a beach ball and Galon was not facing the beach, Aaralyn and Delphia slipped out of the rock face and moved to the fire pit area in the shelter of the giant rock. They quickly undressed themselves and Ronin.

To Galon's shock, they called out to everyone as they waded into the water. Galon didn't know what to do. He was trapped. He tried to not look at his sister and his niece. Delphia quickly approached her uncle, gave him a full body hug and placed her naked son in his arms. She then dove beneath the surface and swam towards Ennis.

Looking back at Galon, she called to him, "Lower yourself and Ronin into the water. He has a surprise for you. In a stunned state, Galon lowered himself and Ronin until they were immersed. To Galon's shock, as soon as Ronin was in the water, he wiggled free of his uncle's embrace and began giggling and cooing as he clumsily swam in circles around a stunned Galen. He called out to Delphia, "O M G! Ronin can swim? How can a baby so young swim?"

Jasper told him, "There is a lot for you to learn about our family. As you can see we all love to be naked a lot. As far as Ronin is concerned, for now, lets just say that Delphia had a water birth, so Ronin's first life experience was in a warm bath. Subsequently he is truly happiest when he is in the water."

After a fun swim time, everyone left the lagoon and headed for the fire pit. Aaralyn had put fluffy towels on the beach chairs to dry off with. As they dried each one took their towels and draped them across the hot rocks. Baby Ronin was the only one who remained snugly wrapped for warmth.

After drying himself on the beach, Galon wrapped his towel around himself and headed for the fire pit. When he rounded the rock, he was shocked to find everyone sitting in lawn chairs, completely naked. They were all enjoying a cold beer. Aaralyn handed Galon a beer as he sat in a chair, still wrapped up. By the time he downed his first beer, Galon stood and said, "What the hell. If you can't beat em, join em." With this statement he whipped his towel off and grabbing another beer; he sat naked in his chair. This brought on a round of cheers and applause from everyone. Jasper thought, 'So far, so good'.

The following week, on Galon's afternoon off, he was prepared for a repeat of their nudist behavior, when Aaralyn told him, "We will have company today. Ennis's mother and her partner will be joining us for a swim, but they can't stay for supper." Seeing the look on her brother's face, she told him, "You have nothing to worry about. They will also be swimming naked. After all we do live next to a massive clothing optional resort area."

Once down on the beach Galon stripped naked, then helped Jasper and Ennis launch the new boat. They held it steady while Aaralyn and Delphia climbed in with baby Ronin. Galon asked, "When will your guests be here?" Ennis told him, Mom and Zeeman will meet us in the lagoon. Oh yes. I don't call her mom. Everyone calls her by her own name, Delja." For a split second, Ennis had to catch himself; he almost used the word sound, instead of name. Once they reached the center of the lagoon, Ennis carefully lowered the anchor. If Galon noticed, he didn't say anything. As always, Ennis was the first to disrobe and dive overboard. He was followed by Jasper, then Aaralyn.

Galon, a bit self conscious, didn't notice that Ennis immediately dove beneath the waves. Galon asked Delphia who was now disrobing herself and Ronin, "Are you sure that this is alright? If everyone is naked, I guess I am OK with being naked too."

She assured Galon, "Yes, we will all be naked. That is our favorite way to be. I must say, though, I am a bit apprehensive. Ennis's mother and her partner are quite different than anyone you have ever met. Just keep an open mind and remember. They are both extremely kind and loving people. They could never wish or do harm to anyone."

Wide eyed and confused, Galon slipped over the side and swam to Ennis. A few minutes later he realized that there were two more swimmers nearby. They swam closer but not too near. Ennis announced, "Galon, I want you to meet my mother, Delja and her partner, Zeeman. They are unable to speak. They do make sounds that translate to feelings. They have been expecting you and are so pleased to meet Aaralyn's brother. Now you remember our habit of greeting and hugging tight even though we are naked? Well, that custom comes from my mother's family. Just remember they are not like us; they live in a different world."

Galon didn't know what to say. He just looked back and forth between Ennis and Delja. Ennis signaled for Delja and Zeeman to come forward to greet Galon. As each in turn grasped him tight and made sounds of happiness as they caressed his back and bottom, he was frozen as if he was a statue. It was obvious that his naked lower half was being pressed against scales rather than male and female flesh.

When he was released, he turned to Ennis, shaking, and asked, "Are those costumes? Do they belong to a group that likes to wear mermaid gear? I have seen that back home. The nearby community pool has a Mer swimming group on Wednesday evenings."

Ennis thought, 'Well, here goes. No turning back now'. He told Galen, "When my father was seventeen he went fishing in his little sailboat. He anchored not too far from his seaside village on the coast of England. That day he met my mother. She fell in love with him. It gave her the courage to break the rules of her people. She enchanted him into the waves and they made love. They spent the entire summer together, swimming and making love.

"I should not have arrived till much later in the fall, once they had moved to their warm winter place. But I did arrive early. I could not have lived with her beneath the waves. Dad took me home that day. He and my grandmother raised me. So there you have it in a nutshell. They do exist and they are beautiful loving people. The folklore of sirens of the sea is just that, folk lore. My mother's people are called Delmar. They are loving, happy and gentle in every way.

"Oh yes, another thing. You have experienced our custom of intimate greeting. My Delmar family do the same. But added to their closeness, they can't help having a curiosity about us land folk.

They call us pillared ones, meaning we stand on pillars. Please don't be offended or take it as being sexual. When they greet you, they often caress your form. You in turn can caress their form to experience the difference from ours. I guess the best way to explain it is to have a demonstration."

Ennis remained close to Galon's side. He sounded to Zeeman that he wanted to have an intimate greeting. Zeeman surged forward and gathered Ennis tightly in his arms. As a wide eyed Galon watched, they slowly swirled around while Ennis ran his hands through Zeeman's hair and caressed his upper body. While Ennis did this, Zeeman sounded happy sounds as he caressed Ennis's upper and lower body. Zeeman caressed Ennis's lower belly in full view of Galen. Seeing the shock on his face, Ennis told him, "I have loved having all my parts caressed by my family. It is their way of sharing the love that I have grown with from birth."

As they parted, Ennis told Galon to look over at the boat. Galen was so shocked he could barely stay afloat as he witnessed Delphia slip naked into the water, then reach into the boat to lift her naked son into the waves. His shock was total when Delphia handed Ronin over to Delja to hold and in return gathered her little newborn Delmar spawn into her arms. Ennis waited a few minutes to let all this sink in. Then he took Galon's arm and urged him forward to meet Delja.

When he reached the group Delphia announced, "Galon, I want you to meet my mother-in-law, Delja and my new Delmar goddaughter, Delphia. Having said this, Delphia and Delja released their charges and watched as the two little ones made happy sounds as they swam in circles together. As soon as her arms were empty,

Delja drew a wide-eyed Galon tightly into her arms and began swirling around while making happy sounds. Galon was too shocked to grasp Delja. He just went with the swirl with his arms at his side. The only sound he made was a loud gasp as Delja ran her hands down his back and caressed his bottom.

After a while, Delphia asked Galon to hold Ronin while she climbed into the boat. She then reached for Ronin. She told Galon, "You can continue to swim with everyone for a while. Another time you will meet more of Ennis's Delmar family. For today, Ronin and I have had enough water and sun. Take your time and enjoy. We can have a good talk about everything over our evening meal."

The rest of the afternoon went well. Ennis told Galon, "As good as we are in the water, you have no idea of the strength that the Delmar have. I inherited two traits from Delja. I can understand and converse with her. Also, my skin is immune to the effects of immersion in sea water. You will see later. Dad will be quite shriveled but my skin will not show any signs that I spent the afternoon in the waves. And, oh, yes, as far as we can tell, I have passed both of my Delmar traits on to Ronin. That is why swimming comes so naturally to him."

The conversation around the fire pit that evening, was very educational for Galon. It was a lot to absorb. Ennis told him, "As long as the ocean is calm, next week on your afternoon off, we will all spend the afternoon in the lagoon. My Delmar family all know about you and now that Delja and Zeeman have met you and are telling them that you are not a threat, they will all want to meet you. It is in their nature to be afraid of us dry land folk

"Just steel yourself to getting used to much more of their curiosity. And please accept being felt all over and enjoy the sensation of feeling their forms. Just remember one important thing. The Delmar remain safe because they remain a part of folk lore. We can never even hint in any way that they do exist. They fear extinction at the hands of the hateful land creatures who slaughtered the gentle whales almost to the point of extinction. They actually do us great service. They guard the beaches and ward off shark attacks. Many surfers without knowing it, have the Delmar to thank for saving their lives. Likewise, when we have horrible storms and boats wreck, they rescue sailors and convey them as close to the land as they can safely do."

Galon slept over that night. He was too shaken to drive back to town. The following week, he came out to visit several evenings. He was filled with questions about the Delmar. By his next day off, Galon was feeling more secure and ready to greet more of Ennis's Delmar family.

The day before, Ennis had sounded to Delja, that on the next light, Galon would be with them. They decided that it was time that he meet more members of the Delmar pod. That afternoon as the entire land family slipped naked from the boat into the lagoon, heads began popping out of the waves. Galon was first introduced to Jennis. Ennis told him that Jennis was the representative of the elders council.

Jennis gathered Galon tightly in his arms while Ennis stayed by their sides translating their greetings. Ennis was pleased that Galon seemed happy to be felt all over by Jennis and in return was exploring Jennis's magnificent form. When they finally parted,

Jennis sounded for all the Delmar present that it was safe to be with Galon.

With that announcement, each Delmar present took turns gathering Galon in their arms while expressing their sounds of happy greetings. A little while later, Jasper spotted Arcelia and Cadao approaching Galon. He thought, 'Oh my, I hope that this goes well'. Galon was a healthy, muscular young male. Jasper had already observed that Galon had experienced a continual succession of painful erections each time that his body had been intimately held and caressed.

Arcelia greeted Galon first. Jasper could see that this greeting took longer than most. He knew why. When she let go of Galon, in a flurry of water, Arcelia surged over to Aaralyn and Delphia. The reason was obvious. Arcelia proudly floated on her back while her friends caressed her very rounded belly. A new Delmar spawn would soon be part of this pair's intimate pod.

Looking back over the grouping, Jasper noticed that Galon and Cadao still remained locked together in greeting. But strangely, they were slowly rotating and drifting further away from the gathering. At that point, Aaralyn called Jasper over. She asked him to watch Ronin and keep him safe while he swam in his usual circles. She then moved off with several of the Delmar females for a private time. Every once in a while, she called out to Ennis to please translate sounds for her. Jasper was so intent watching Ronin have a happy time, that he didn't notice how long Galon spent off in a distance with Cadao.

That evening, an exhausted gathering sat around the fire pit enjoying glasses of wine and beer as they digested their fire-cooked meal. A happy and exhausted Ronin, swaddled in a large beach towel, slept soundly in his mother's arms. Jasper was so pleased that the day's events had been successful. Their family had now officially expanded and all was well. He didn't notice that Galon was acting a bit coy, when talking about their afternoon in the lagoon.

Aaralyn though, did notice his behavior. She addressed Galon, "Galon, You spent a long time off with Cadao today. You are my brother. I know you all too well. Is there something that you want to tell us? We only have each other. Growing up we never had secrets that we didn't share. I have a feeling that you actually had an intimate experience with Cadao. And you are also harboring a secret that you have not shared with me. Our openness is why I wasted no time in sharing my love for nudity and opening your mind to the fact that we now have, 'Unique' in-laws. So keeping in mind that we all love you, Fess up."

Sheepishly looking downward like a little boy in trouble, Galon spoke, "Well sis, as always you are right. I can't keep a secret from you. When it comes to observing me, you have X-ray vision. I did spend a lot of time with Cadao. He is a magnificent male. It started with the hugging and feeling about, like all the other Delmar did. But I couldn't help myself. When he realized that I was rigid with sexual excitement, it started. He grabbed my manhood and placed his full erection in my hands. It was amazing. I have never had such a sensuous experience in my life.

"I won't share details, but suffice to say we did it all. Now I feel guilty. I have to confess. I intended to tell you as soon as I could get up the nerve. It was easy to keep my secret from you when I lived half a world away. But now I can't hide any more. I have been gay and out for several years now. Having said that, I now have an issue that I will need help with. As you know, I brought two of my staff here with me. In fact, one is more than staff. Alonzo and I have been together for five years now. I hope that he can become part of your extended family. We do have a monogamous relationship. That is why I am feeling so guilty about what happened today. It was just the shock of everything that has happened; it weakened my resolve. Being held in Cadao's arms while having his hands explore my private parts made me lose control. And when he presented me with his manhood, it was game over for me."

Jasper and Aaralyn immediately rose from their beach chairs, walked over to Galon and gathered him into their arms. Jasper told him, "If you love Alonzo, that is wonderful. As far as our Delmar family goes, let's take it in steps, like we did with you. He asked, Does Alonzo have hangups about public nudity?"

Galon assured him, "No. We often go to clothing optional beaches and resorts. Granted most that we frequent are gay only. But there is a beach near Vancouver where both sexes enjoy nudity. We hang out there a lot in the summer. I agree, that is, we should introduce him slowly to family nudity, like you did with me. Back home it was easy to be on a nude beach, because other than a couple of friends, everyone was a stranger. This situation is different, in that we are all an intimate family group. Having said that, I believe that it should go well. Alonzo is a kind and honest man. I love him dearly. I am sure that he will be able to handle the shock of being naked and meeting your Delmar family. As for Cadao. I believe that he will respond as I did. He is a horny man and only human. I will be by his side, so if it does get sexual, he will know that I approve."

31

The following week Galon and Alonzo came for a visit. Jasper and Aaralyn set everything up as they did with Galon. Alonzo had no problem with stripping and joining Jasper and Ennis as they frolicked in the surf. Like Galon had, he became wide-eyed when Aaralyn, Delphia and baby Ronin joined them naked. In a while he relaxed and they had a good afternoon and evening. When they left the fireside to head back to town he was quite amazed as each one in turn held him naked and tight as they welcomed him to the family and bid him goodnight.

That week, he and Galon talked a lot. Galon didn't actually admit to the existence of the Delmar, but he did prepare Alonzo for the fact that Aaralyn's extended family were all nudists. He emphasized that they were also very tactile and familiar when greeting new family that they felt safe in trusting

The following gathering in the lagoon was an interesting day. It started as the previous one with Galon had. Alonzo hesitantly disrobed and slid into the water with the rest of their family. Once he was in the water, Jasper and Galon remained by his side. Jasper told him, "You are about to meet Ennis's mother, Delja and her partner, Zeeman. They are like, and unlike us. But please relax and keep an open mind. They are bodily tactile and nudists like we are. So please, just take it as it comes. I promise, you will be perfectly safe and you will learn amazing things today. Galon has learned it already but it can't be explained. The only way is to learn in person. Just be aware that when they greet you, they are both unable to speak. They can only make limited sounds."

That afternoon went well. Alonzo, with Galon constantly at his side, weathered the shock reasonably well. Galon and Jasper were pleased that today, Arcelia and Cadao were not present. Both thought, 'That would be an experience for another day'. At least, by then, Alonzo will be more relaxed and better prepared to cope with their level of intimacy.

Two weeks later the lagoon gathering included Arcelia and Cadao. Jasper and Aaralyn observed, when after a while, Cadao drifted off with Galon and Alonzo in tow. Later, when they returned to the grouping Ennis and Jasper swam over to Galon and Alonzo. Grasping the pair tight, body to body in an intimate three-way hug, Ennis told Alonzo, "I hope that all went well with your time with Cadao. I know it's strange to us land folk. But my Delmar family and all Delmar have the same traditions. They do have intimate and permanent life and mating partners. But when it comes to sensuality and sex, they are by tradition different. A sexual encounter between friends has no meaning beyond that of sharing and cementing close friendship. Should either of you have a sexual experience with Cadao or any other Delmar male, remember that it is the best expression of friendship that they know.

"I am only warning you and Galon. There will be Delmar females who are overly curious. Be careful. To be explored and caressed is safe, but to have a sexual experience with a Delmar female could, all too easily end up in producing a new life. They are extremely prolific. That is what happened years ago with my dad and Delja. It's a miracle that I was born early and was able to be immediately cared for by Dad and my Nan. They expected I would be born a Delmar. Had I arrived deep in the ocean, I would have died. You will learn soon enough what Delmar traits I have inherited from Delja and have passed on to Ronin."

That evening, Alonzo hugged bodily tight and said good night to everyone. Jasper and Aaralyn were so pleased that it had all gone well. Two weeks later, when everyone was in the lagoon for an afternoon gathering with their Delmar family, they had special visitors. Keone and Nadish appeared with Trai and Kato in tow. Jasper and Ennis were so surprised. They had not seen the identical twins since they were babes-in-arms. Jasper figured that they were now about eight cycles old. When they enjoyed a welcoming embrace, it was obvious. As they matured, they remained identical. They were now happy and extremely handsome Delmar youth.

As Jasper introduced Keone and Nadish along with their sons, each in turn bodily greeted Galon and Alonzo, Jasper told the story of their youth and growing into an intimate family pod. Hearing this story enlightened Galon and Alonzo. That evening at the fire-pit gathering, they confessed their feelings to everyone. Galon admitted to his family group, "Meeting Keone and Nadish today was amazing for us both. To realize that the Delmar have and accept gay coupling is wonderful. The added miracle is that they accept that gay couples should also raise children, or I guess you call their little ones spawn. That is totally enlightening.

"We were waiting for the right time to tell you all. There is an orphanage in town. They have so many children who need to be loved. We have applied to adopt a young brother and sister who were abandoned a year ago, when they were six months and two. We both hope that you all will support us in this venture. God knows we know little about parenting. We will depend on our family for both assistance and advice."

Once hugs and happiness was shared by all, holding Jasper's hand, Aaralyn made an announcement. "Well this is an amazing development. I can assure you both that we are more than happy for you. We will always be on hand to help in any way possible. With that in mind, we now have an urgent task. Jasper agrees with me. We will take the plans we used for the two bedroom cottage that we built for Ennis and Delphia and expand it to be a three bedroom cottage. We had decided that it was doable in case Ennis and Delphia had a second child. Daughters and sons should have their own room to grow up in. I already have the spot picked out that I was planning to offer to Galon. Now it will be a family home. We are all so pleased." With this announcement, everyone gathered in a huddle around Galon and Alonzo to celebrate their coming together as a family.

32

The following month Jasper rented a back-hoe and electric cement mixer. He also ordered several loads of rock and heavy timbers. It would expedite the process of construction for Galon and Alonzo's cottage. Time was of the essence. They had rented a two bedroom furnished flat in town in anticipation of their new son and daughter's arrival. Rather than hiring strangers to work, they paid an extra generous hourly rate to have the entire dive team help out in their spare time. They were all appreciative of the pay.

In just one month the rock walls were up and solid. Two of the local divers had previously worked in construction. They were invaluable in helping to frame the interior and the assembling of roof rafters. As the fourth month of construction ended, a grand housewarming party was planned. Jasper and Aaralyn would have loved to make it a beach party, but everyone agreed that their special access to the cove below the cliffs, had to be kept secret. Like their

Delmar family, the private beach and the treasure hidden deep in the cliff could not be revealed.

Three months later, Jasper had an idea to discuss. He proposed a trip for Ennis, Delphia, Ronin, Aaralyn and himself. It was for an upcoming anniversary of his mother's death. He wished to visit his parents' grave and also the place where he grew up. He also proposed an additional plan. Sitting around their private fire pit he explained it all. "We have talked about going to England for a trip so that Aaralyn and Delphia could see where we came from. I have heard from friends that my parent's old home is being used as a vacation rental, or, as we call it in England, 'A Vacation Let'. It is doing well, because it overlooks the harbor. It's built there by tradition. My father was a fisherman. Most fishermen in the past built their cottages near the wharf where they kept their boats.

I also have a secondary plan. My best friend growing up was Clifford. He now owns the jewelry store and I hear is an excellent craftsman. His father was the village jeweler. He has obviously taken over from him. If everyone is in agreement, we will select a necklace or jewel-encrusted broach to take to him. We can tell him that we found it washed up on the shore after a violent storm. I trust my friend completely. If all goes well, from time to time, Aaralyn and I will return to England for a visit and do business with Clifford. We will never be able to chance having a show of wealth. But, because our family and little private community are growing, it will be good to have some extra financial security tucked away."

Everyone agreed with Jasper's plan. The following month they all flew to England. It was summer there, so Jasper knew that their Delmar family would be nearby. Once they were settled in his family home, he went to the harbor and rented a sail boat. Three days later the dawn broke on a beautiful, warm sunny day. Everyone climbed into the boat and sailed off for a day on the water.

As soon as they reached the area where their Delmar family love day always happened, Ennis stripped naked and dove into the water. After spending so long in their semi-tropical place, it was a shock to him. He had forgotten that the warm summer water off the coast of England was not nearly as warm as the water by their new home. Before he resurfaced, he called out several times for his Delmar family. He repeated this process every half hour. Shortly after his third try, a head appeared. They were all pleased to see that it was Zeeman. He sounded to Ennis that news had spread among the Delmar that someone was calling them. No one was willing to investigate, because they were not expecting anyone.

Zeeman was overjoyed when he realized who was in the boat. After hugging and greeting Ennis, he dove deep to announce to all, that their pillared family had arrived. In no time, they were surrounded by a gathering of Delmar. The water there was too deep to secure a line to the bottom. Jasper had a solution that allowed everyone to enter the water. He tied the line around his waist. It just meant that he had to stay within reach of Zeeman in case the wind forced the boat away, dragging him with it. Jasper was happy being around his Delmar family, and also being in the arms of his two loves, Delja and Zeeman.

At one point Jennis arrived to check that all was well. He stayed a while and had a long conference with Ennis. Later that afternoon, they all bid farewell to their Delmar family. It would only be four to six weeks before they were together again in their warm place, near their new homes.

That evening after their meal they all settled for a chat. Ennis had an announcement. He told everyone, "I had a long talk with Jennis today. I told him why we were here. He is a brilliant thinker, I'm sure that is why he was chosen to be an elder at such a young age. He sounded to me that a way down the coast from their resting place near our homes, there is a similar gathering of pillared one's resting places, with busy surf beaches like the one near us. He sounded that it had been on the list of possible birthing places, but they had chosen their present location because it afforded greater safety.

"The reason for talking about this place, is that not too far off shore, there is a series of reefs. Scattered around one of those reefs, there is an ancient sailing ship. Jennis tells me that it has all but been consumed by the burrowing creatures. He also tells me that this wreck has a small amount of treasure aboard. He suggested that if we are planning to claim the treasure that we wish to sell, we say we found it diving in the shallow waters off that beach, rather than in the area of our home. That way, we would be adding another layer of security to our hiding place, and also for our Delmar family and their nearby birthing place."

Everyone agreed that this was a good idea. The following day Aaralyn and Jasper went to the jeweler's shop to meet with Clifford. It went well. Clifford suggested that he dismantle the jewel-encrusted broaches, then re-work the gold into rings and broaches for each individual stone. He trusted his old friend Jasper and agreed that he would be hounded for the location of the find if it was kept in its original shape. Jasper promised Clifford that from time to time he would continue to explore around that reef to try and find more pieces. That left the door open for selling more gems, should they ever need a further infusion of funds.

When they returned to their homes on the cliff, they came up with a plan. Jasper invited Galon, Alonzo and their children over for a homecoming meal. After the meal was finished, Jasper opened a fresh bottle of wine and made an announcement. "As you know, we recently made a trip back to England to visit my old home. It was great to actually be able to stay in my parent's house. It's now a holiday rental.

"I had another reason to return there. I had heard from my parent's lawyer. I guess I was too young to be aware of what went on, when my father died. His fishing boat was quite new and of a good size. Mom had sold it and put the funds along with his life insurance money into a trust investment account in my name. She probably intended to tell me about it when I got older, but time has a way of slipping by. I took good care of Mom, so I am sure she never thought of needing that money. In the end she was quite confused but happy. Her memory of my childhood remained reasonably sharp, but her memory of anything recent or practical had faded.

"So now we come to the present. We are not rich, but thanks to Mom and Dad, we do have a nest egg. I talked it over with Aaralyn and we have at least an immediate plan. This week Galon and I will go to town together. We will tell the auto dealer that I inherited a bit of money from my parents in England. Aaralyn's old truck is barely running. The mechanic has been warning us for a while that he is running out of ways to resuscitate it. Owning this property, we do need a truck. We will buy a near new car for us, a nearly new SUV for Galon and Alonzo, and a good late model used truck for us all to use. I had thought of possibly buying a van for Galon, but the dive shop already has a nearly new passenger van that is used to haul divers and equipment back and forth to the beaches."

Everyone was happy with this announcement. The following week Aaralyn accompanied Galon and Jasper to the dealerships. To make their story more believable she made a fuss over the colors of the vehicles. She told each salesman, "God knows when we will ever be able to buy another vehicle. This one has to be right in both size and color so that I will be satisfied for a long while. We have no one else in our family that will leave us a windfall." That statement made it clear that they were paying cash for the vehicles with a small inheritance.

Galon and Alonzo's new family settled in right away. They were too young to remember another way of life. The baby boy was called Carlos. His slightly older sister Maria, fussed over him like he was her own child. Aaralyn and Delphia took turns caring for them while their fathers were at work. Delphia took care on all the days that Aaralyn worked at the dive shop. After the first busy season, they came up with a new plan. There was no question of having help at home. That would compromise their privacy and lifestyle. Aaralyn found a young single mother who lived with her parents. Annette had a community college business degree. She could have gotten a better job by going away to the city. But with two small ones to care for, she needed to stay in her parent's home.

It all worked out well. She loved working in the dive shop, and because she had her parents to care for her children, she was easily able to fill in for Aaralyn on an almost-full-time basis.

Three months later, Aaralyn started to notice that Annette was showing up for work dressed just a little nicer. She was also taking more care with her makeup and hair. One evening by the fire pit, Aaralyn happened to mentioned this to Galon and Alonzo. Both men immediately broke into laughter. Galon told her, "O M G sis. Are you slipping in your old age? What happened to your X-ray vision? You are right in what is happening with Annette's appearance. But you have somehow missed the why.

"Watch her next time our head dive instructor, Antonio, comes into the shop. She lights up like a Christmas tree. I can also tell you that Antonio absolutely basks in her glow. He even goes to her parents now for Sunday dinners. I figure it is just a matter of time before we have to host a wedding."

Aaralyn admitted, "Well, maybe I am slipping. I need to smarten up my act, for sure. But I must admit, Antonio is a good man. I think that he will make Annette and her children happy."

Four months later, Galen's prediction came true. Everyone was on hand at the local church to witness the marriage of Antonio and Annette. When they returned from their honeymoon, Annette decided that she wanted to continue working with Aaralyn. That made everyone in the dive center happy.

One week, a funny thing happened. Being peak season, they were all running flat out. One of the tourists, a blond shapely middle-aged woman from Portugal, approached Annette. She requested that instead of the dive instructor that she had today, she wanted to have Antonio tomorrow. She had no shame in telling Annette that she thought he was the hottest of the team and she wanted to get wet with him.

Annette assured the woman that she would see what she could arrange. The following morning when the woman arrived, she was greeted by a large framed wedding portrait of Annette and Antonio posing with the two children. It was prominently perched on the counter beside the cash register. From that day on everyone teased Antonio about that situation.

The seasons ran one into another. Everyone in their pillared and Delmar family stayed well. Carlos and Maria had never been exposed to water and swimming. As they grew, they came to love being in the cove and before long were introduced to their Delmar relatives. They and their spawn cousins continued to grow and flourish. Because Delphia had a teacher's certificate, they built a small classroom in the garden. By the time all the children had to move on to high school, they would all be old enough to understand the danger of revealing the existence of their unique relatives.

Not a lot changed as far as Jasper's attempt to convince the world that they were destroying the oceans, but he never gave up trying. Ennis continued to coordinate with Jennis in order to keep the Delmar safe.

Three full cycles later there was an important event. On a clear and calm day, Jasper, Ennis, Galon, Alonzo and their entire family entered the warm waters. Jennis had requested that they all be present. No one on land knew what was happening. As soon as they were immersed, heads started to appear. But this day, it was not just their usual assortment of Delmar playmates. The Delmar gathering formed a large circle, drawing their land family into their midst. Suddenly within the circle, twenty more heads appeared. Jennis surfaced at the head of the inner gathering. He sounded to Ennis to please tell his pod that the new visitors were representatives from their governing council of elders.

Ennis translated this to his family, then looked questioningly over to the group of elders. Immediately Jennis flowed forward with a female elder at his side. Together they grasped Ennis's hands and drew him towards the elders group.

Jennis sounded that Taras was the head of the elders' council. Then he sounded that the council had made a decision that would be a first for all Delmar pods. Ennis would, from that day on, become an elder of their pod. As he sounded this amazing news, Ronin translated for his shocked family. Following the ceremony, it took the rest of the afternoon for each member of Jasper's 'pillared one's' pod to meet and intimately greet the entire assembly.

The End

About the author

Nino Balistreri was born and spent his younger years in Barrie Ontario. He attended high school in North Bay, Ontario. As a teen he lived with an aunt in Chicago for two years. He studied social work and lived in Toronto and Ottawa before his love of the ocean drew him to the East Coast. Being of Sicilian heritage and coming from the cold of Ontario, Nino has a love of tropical climes. He enjoys his winter writing time in both Florida and Hawaii.

As a child Nino felt removed from both his family and the religious society that taught and abused him. His only safe place in life was to create a fantasy world where he could be nurtured and unconditionally loved. Constantly escaping to his own world gave him a reason to live. It helped him to survive till adulthood.

As an adult Nino was famous for entertaining his friends with never-ending tales. He could expand the simplest of happenings into a too lengthy account. By his mid forties Nino realized that his own fantasies could be translated into fiction and adventure stories.

Thanks to professional tutoring, he was able to format his ideas into print. His first three books, Death's Secret, Anchorage of

Gold and Danger Cave were published by Create Space which became Kindle Publishing. He also contributed to Salt and Wild a compilation of Shelburne NS writers. It was published by Boularderie Island Press. A Florida based detective novel titled Lauderdale Tales is now available along with all of his books on Amazon Books as well as online with Cole's, Indigo and Chapters. This publication of Delmar of the Deeps will be followed by Becoming Michael and a seven-part vampire series titled Blood Lust.

Nino belongs to The Writers Federation of Nova Scotia and when in Florida attends Pine Island Writers.

Delmar of the Deeps

Name Sources
- mernetwork.com
- meaningofnames.com
- nameberry.com

Delmar – Spanish – Of the Sea
Yahaira – Arabian – Jewell
Bahari – African – Sea Man
Jennis – American – Wild Wave
Larina – Latin American – Seagull
Lanikai – American – Heavenly Sea
Lulwa – Arabic – Pearl
Shui – Chinese – Coming from Water
Taras – Greek/Russian - Poseidon's Son
Gazsi – Hungarian/Persian – King of the Treasure
Marella – Irish/Celtic – Shining Sea
Keone – Hawaiian – The Sand
Nadish – Indian – The Sea
Negeen – Persian – Gem
Galia – Hebrew – Born in Waves
Delja – Polish – Daughter of the Sea
Zeeman – Dutch – Sea Man
Jasper – Hebrew – Jewel
Ennis – Irish – From the Island
Kye – American – Ocean
Zamir – Arabic/Hebrew – Beautiful Voice/Song

Varun – Indian – Lord of the Sea
Dylon – England – Son of the Sea
Tamaki – Japanese – Jewel/Gem
Marino – Latin American – Of the Sea
Gryta – Greek – Pearl
Cephas – Aramaic – Rock
Trai – Vietnamese - Oyster
Kato – Bantu – Second Twin
Kawai – Hawaiian – Coming from Water
Almeta – African – Born of God
Rodion – Russian – Song of the Hero
Matsya – India Fish
Gryta – Greek – Pearl
Arcelia – Spanish – Treasure Chest
Cadao – Vietnamese - Song
Ephyra – Latin America – Daughter of Oceanus
Llyr – Welsh – God of the Sea
Aaralyn – America Song
Delphia – Spanish – Dolphin
Galon – Hebrew a Strong Wave
Ronin – Japanese – Lone Samurai

Manufactured by Amazon.ca
Bolton, ON

35294735R00125